DADDY DEVIL

D, Dante, DB, Whisperdevil. You wear many name hats, but to me? To me, you are Batman... or a ninjaing baby giraffe... Or a lady of the night...

You are a weirdo that prefers the cold, I am a weirdo that prefers the heat. You are a giant, I am a midget... You are the ying to my yang. Thanks for being a good cunt. You go alright. Peace out mutha-flipper!

TRIGGER WARNING

This book contains graphic scenes. These scenes range from rape, mental and physical abuse and sexual intercourse. Some scenes are BDSM related.

CHAPTER 1

Damian's POV
SEXUAL CONTENT **18+**

Sitting at the small round table in the window of the little cafe across the road, lightning cracks the sky sending Heaven's light through the gloomy clouds that perfectly match my mood. I trace my finger around the top of the takeaway coffee cup, warming my icy hands. I stare at the grey coloured highrise on the other side of the street and wonder if I actually have to go in today. I *am* the CEO, after all. I'm sure I can give myself permission to take a day off, but what would I do? It's a foreign concept to the corporate world. I work all the time.

A loud shattering sound brings me back to reality. Turning towards the raucous, I see the cute little waitress, the one I've ogled many times over the last six months. I'm sitting there taking in the sight of her - even tied back, her long brown hair flowing over her shoulders. She crouches down to pick up the bits of broken cup that are scattered all over the floor. Her black ripped skinny jeans pull hard around her ass as she squats down to clear the mess, her dark shitkickers covered in the liquid from the mug.

Hearing her apologise to the man as she works to clean

the mess, she stumbles over her words like she is about to let her emotions get the better of her. I look at the man in the seat next to where she is and notice his face turning red with increasing rage. I watch as his hands clench into fists on the table, not even trying to hide his anger. In an instant he was on his feet, sending the chair he was sitting on flying backwards hitting the customer at the table close by without any regard for the rest of the cafe.

"What the fuck do you think you are doing, you stupid bitch? Look what you've done! You have spilled coffee everywhere!" His hands flap around exaggerated by his increased anger. "Go back over there and make me a new one, for fucks sake!" He curses as his giant frame towers over her tiny one, an obvious move to intimidate her.

And that is all I need to hear. *Asshole, you don't talk to a woman like that.*

Jumping up and stalking over to the 'man,' I put myself between him and the waitress, making sure I'm creating distance, putting my hands up in front of me to show I'm just trying to calm the situation.

"Hey, buddy. It was an accident, how about you back off, let her clean up the mess and get you a new coffee? She already apologised and is trying to fix the situation," I said, as I move myself and the waitress back.

"How about you mind your own fucking business, *buddy.*" he retorts, poking a finger in my chest.

Standing at six foot five inches, I tower over the man. I have to give him credit for trying to square me up. I mean, he is barely 6 foot tall, and not nearly as well defined as I am. So much so, his white button-up shirt is gaping between the buttons, his crinkled tie doing a terrible job of hiding it and his buxom belly hanging over his black slacks.

"I'm sorry, I can't just stand by while you abuse a woman for an accident. Who do you think you are to speak to her that way? This woman deserves respect, not your abuse." I'm starting to get agitated, so I pull my wallet out of my pocket and try to hand the man $100. "Here, I expect this will cover the coffee. Now let me escort you out. There's a little coffee shop around the corner, maybe go there from now on," I say to him as I guide him, much to his annoyance, through the door and wave him off.

Turning around, I see the waitress staring at me, tears falling down her face. I carefully move back towards her, not wanting to heighten her fear. "Miss, are you okay? Did he actually touch you?" I guide her to my table and help her to sit down, pouring a glass of water.

"I can't. I can't sit. I.. I.. I have to work." She stumbles over her words and gets up from the chair. But, I stop her by carefully taking her wrist, easing her back down into the chair.

"Please," I say, "If your boss has a problem he can talk to me." I take a seat next to her at the table and hold my hand out. "Hi, I'm Damian."

Tentatively, she returns the gesture, shaking my hand, "Hi, I'm Leah. It's a pleasure to meet you."

"Are you going to be okay today? You're trembling." I point to her hands holding the glass of water.

"I'll be fine, honestly. He shook me up a little, that's all." She shakes her head dismissively, as if trying to convince herself she was alright.

I go to ask Leah if she has anyone to pick her up, but I'm interrupted by my phone ringing.

"Sorry, I have to get this, it's my office." I watch as she nods at me and gives me a weak smile.

Answering the call. "Yeah?" I pause, hearing the panicked

voice of my assistant, "What? Oh God, Fuck! Okay, I'll be right there. Okay. Thanks, Maria. Bye."

Hanging up, I look over at Leah, "Sorry, I have to go, office emergency." I stand up and walk off, stopping and turning to look back at the woman, "Hope to see you again, Leah." I wink at her and walk out the door.

My pace increases to a light jog as I cross the road to my office building. I push through the front doors and my pace quickens as I head to the elevators. Pressing the button to go up, I take my phone out and start scrolling through social media, constantly seeing pictures of myself out and about. I shake my head and let out a sigh as I come across the picture of me helping the guy from the cafe out.

Hearing the ding of the elevator, I step through the doors and enter, pressing the button for the top floor.

The god awful elevator music reminds me to talk to maintenance and have them change it to something more... modern.

The doors slide open and I see the hustle and bustle of the offices. Maria, my Personal Assistant, rushes up to me as I step out.

"I'm so sorry, sir. She just walked into your office and won't leave." Maria starts to fuss, the panic in her voice blatant. "I didn't know what to do. That's why I called."

"It's okay, Maria. You did the right thing. I'll deal with it," I assure her, stalking towards my office door with a scowl on my face. *She is the last person I want to see!*

Hurriedly, I wrench the door open, and I see her sitting there - on my desk - grinning at me like she has any business being here.

"Hey, baby." She drawls at me. While her intention was

to be sexy, the words came out vile, like venom dripping from her mouth.

"Marisha, do not call me baby. We aren't together anymore, we haven't been for months. Leave, now!"

Slinking off the desk, she stalks across my office, wrapping her sickly long nails around my tie and tries to pull me in for a kiss. I was fast to wrench away as I spoke, "What the fuck, Marisha." I grip her arms and push her back to create distance. "Get off me!" I spoke in measured out syllables.

"C'mon baby, you know nobody will love you like I can." She drops to her knees, the desperate servant she is as she starts unzipping my suit pants.

Looking me in the eyes as she strokes my dick through my grey boxer, I can't help but groan as I react to her sensitive touch. Marisha takes that as a sign that she can keep going and pulls my dick out of my boxers, taking my semi hard cock into her mouth.

Aggressively, I grab her hair in my fist and pull my dick out of her mouth... before slamming it back in just as forcefully. Grabbing her hair in my fist, I pull my dick out of her mouth before slamming myself back in again. I know better than to encourage her, but my cock betrays me as I work quickly to get myself off. I listen to her gag and gurgle as I pump in and out, the sounds turning me on.

"That's it, you whore. Take that big cock." I slam into her eager mouth harder, without care or regard. "Fuck, I'm going to come already and you are going to swallow everything I give you, then you are going to fuck off out of my office and my life," I say as I thrust harder and faster, groaning as I finally come, with my dick deeply penetrating her throat.

After I've emptied myself into her, I straighten myself up, quickly zipping my fly on my trousers, and chucking her a couple of tissues from my desk.

"Here, take these. Wipe your mouth and fuck off."

As she takes them and cleans herself up, I can tell she's about to say something. I cut her off before she gets the chance. "I said leave, Marisha! What just happened was because I needed to get off and you were keen... nothing else. Stop calling and coming round," I give her a steely gaze as I speak my final words, "I don't want you!"

She stomps her way over to the door. "You're an asshole, Damian!" Throwing the door open and leaving in a huff, she pushes my staff out of her way as she goes.

How the fuck did I ever date her? She's a vile person with no heart for others.

I look at Maria, who's shaking her head while she watches my ex leave the floor. "I don't know what you ever saw in her, Sir."

"Me either, Maria... Me either." I reply as I close the door and sit behind my desk, my thoughts drifting back to the waitress, Leah.

CHAPTER 2

Damian's POV

Sitting behind my desk, I have my head in my hands, taking deep breaths. It's been hours since the Marisha incident. *What the fuck was I thinking? Now Marisha will never leave me alone. What the fuck have I done?*

The knock on my door pulls me back to the present. Looking towards the door, I speak out, "yeah."

Maria pokes her head through the small opening. "Sorry to disturb you, sir. I have a Miss Williams here for the personal assistant position. Would you like me to send her in?"

I look up at her, "Yes please, Maria. And if you could join us, please. I need to make sure the two of you gel, as well as with me, so go get her and get someone else to bring the three of us coffees, please."

She nods at me and walks out the door, leaving it slightly ajar.

Within a minute, Maria is walking through with Leah, the last person I expected to see in my office.

I stand up to greet her, "Leah?" She's looking at me, stunned. She obviously didn't expect to see me here either.

Maria is just looking between the two of us, confused. "I'm sorry, sir. Do you two know each other?"

As hard as it is, I manage to take my eyes off of Leah and turn to Maria. "Um, we met this morning when she was working at the cafe across the street. Some jackass abused her for dropping his coffee. Cunt..."

"Damian!" Maria is quick to chastise me, "There is a lady in your presence. You do not say such things!" I lower my head. This woman is like my mother and has no problem scolding me when she thinks I need it.

"Sorry, Maria. But really, he was," I add quickly in my own defence. "You should have heard the horrible things he was saying about her... to her!"

Maria looks at me, "I want you to apologise to Miss Winters, right now!"

I look at Leah. I see her grinning at me and I know she's enjoying this.

"I apologise, Leah." I hear Maria clear her throat. "I mean, Miss Winters. Please, let's take a seat so we can get this interview started."

Taking in a deep breath before slowly blowing it out, I glance at Leah, really look at her, and realise she's absolutely stunning. I notice she's staring at me, and it's not just her. Maria is too.

Did they ask me something? Just play it cool, Damian.

"I'm sorry, what was that?" They both start to smile and giggle.

Maria is the one to speak. "Good lord, Mr. Caldwell! You are a disaster after you know who left.' Maria says as she shakes her head in disapproval before continuing, "How about I go chase up our coffees and you can get the interview started?"

She wants to leave me here alone with Leah? Fucking hell.

Leah watches as Maria walks out the door, closing it behind her. "Well, that wasn't very subtle, was it?" she laughs out.

"I love Maria, she's like a mother to me. But no, she's anything but subtle." I laugh back and look down at the floor, unaware that Leah hasn't taken her eyes away from me.

"So, Mr. Caldwell. Where would you like to start?" mischief swirling in her eyes.

Without thinking I instantly reply, "Dinner." I can tell that I've caught her by surprise with my request.

"Agh," she starts stumbling over her words. "Um, I don't think that is appropriate. Not if I'm going for a job as your personal assistant."

I drop my head. No woman has ever turned me down before. This is uncharted territory for me. "Fine, you have the job. How about a celebratory dinner? Maria can join us. You know, so we can all get to know each other. We will be working very closely. I have a few things coming up that will require the three of us to be working long hours together; potentially overnighters."

She starts nodding at me, not really understanding how much time we are going to be spending together.

"So, would you like the job?" I ask her as Maria walks back in with our coffees. I watch as she looks at Maria who nods her head.

"Really?" her shock is obvious before she continues, "that would be amazing, thank you."

I turn to Maria, "Can you please book a table for the three of us for tonight at my usual restaurant." She looks at me, "Um, Mr Caldwell. I won't be able to make it, but I can book the table for the two of you if you would like me to, sir?"

"Yes, please. Make it for seven-thirty?" I turn to Leah. "If that's suitable for you?" I question her, hoping she says yes.

Leah is looking at me, stunned. "Yes," she complies quietly, almost a whisper. "That's fine. Um, I only had a movie night planned with my housemate, but I can call and let him know I have to go out tonight."

Hearing her say her housemate was a 'he' pissed me off to no end. I can't let her see that though, she needs to think this will be purely business.

"Fantastic! So I'll get the driver to pick you up at seven and we will head to the restaurant." I say to her, directing Leah to stand. "Now, I have a lot of work to do before tonight, so if you will excuse me, I have to go. Maria will walk you through all the paperwork and take you down to HR for a staff pass to get into the building." I start walking her to the door.

Stopping just outside the door she turns to me. "I'll see you tonight, Damian... Ah, I mean, Mr Caldwell." I laugh at her shaking my head.

"I will see you tonight at seven, Oh and until the paperwork is signed, it's Damian." I smile at her. Shutting the door as she walks away, I lean my forehead on it. *What the hell am I doing? Taking Leah on a not date... date. Fuck! Ok, this is going to be interesting,* I think as I walk back to sit behind my desk, pulling out the pile of contracts I have to read through. *This was the worst idea I've ever had.*

CHAPTER 3

Leah's POV

Putting the last of my makeup on, I wonder if Damian understands this isn't a date. I can't date my boss, especially one who's just hired me, but I have a feeling he may be taking this as a date.

Glancing over at the clock I see it's already six fifty-five pm. "Okay, If Damian is anything, he is most likely always on time," I say to myself just as the doorbell rings.

"Shit! Okay, I can do this." I give myself a quick pep talk. "He's going to be your boss, no silly behaviour, Leah," I tell myself in the mirror as I straighten out my well fitted red satin dress. *He sure is good looking though, which makes it harder to stay away for sure.*

Making my way to the door, I open it up to see someone I don't know standing on my front porch.

"Hello?" I say, kind of quizzing them at the same time.

"Hi, Miss Williams. I'm Mr. Caldwell's driver. We have come to pick you up." He states.

Staring at him blankly. "Okay, if he's in the car, why didn't he come to the door?" I say rolling my eyes.

The man just smiles at me and leads me outside, before leaning closer to me and saying, "Mr Caldwell likes the bratty ones."

I look up at the man confused. "Excuse me, I'm a grown woman. I'm no brat, Thank you very much."

He starts laughing as he opens the car door for me. Sliding in the backseat I see Damian as the driver looks at him. "She's an innocent one, Sir. Don't know if she can handle it."

I scoff at him as Damian laughs and I notice his canine teeth are sharpened, like a vampire. "It's not like that, she's my new PA alongside Maria. Maria was meant to be joining us tonight but unfortunately couldn't."

Being satisfied with that answer the driver jumps in the front, putting up the divider of the SUV.

I whip my head to look at Damian, "Um, why did your driver call me a brat? And why did he say you like them? I don't understand."

Is he smiling at me? Is he fucking smiling at me? "Did I say something that amuses you, Mr Caldwell?"

"We aren't at the office, you can call me Damian." He replies, not answering my question.

"No, thank you. I'd like to keep it professional." I now notice just how handsome he is in his black suit which is paired with a red button-up shirt and black tie, accompanied with black suspenders. It should be illegal how good he looks - he's making my knees weak. Damian continues to smirk at me like he knows what he's doing to my body.

"You're staring at me, Leah. Is there something you want to say?" He asks in a husky voice while raising an eyebrow at me.

I shake my head at him. I can't let him know the effect he has on me with just one look.

Sitting in silence for the rest of the car ride was awkward to say the least. That isn't to say I wasn't aware of the constant glances from Damian, heating my skin as I continue to look out the window with nervous tension.

Pulling into the restaurant carpark, Damian gets out while the driver opens the door for me.

Following, I see Damian standing there, arm out ready for me to loop mine through. *He's being such a gentleman, I wonder if he's always like this?* I think to myself as I take what he's offered me.

Walking through the front door, I hear Damian talking to the waitress. Looking around the restaurant, I see that the eyes of all the women are focused on me... or is it Damian. I realise it is definitely me when I notice their faces all wearing the same look of disgust, their disdain not even hidden in the slightest.

Damian walks up behind me and wraps his arm around my waist, whispering in my ear. "They are jealous of you. You are beautiful, Leah."

I straighten up, as I assist Damian in removing his hand from me, "This is business, Mr Caldwell. You can remove your arm now." *I want him to leave it there, though I can't let him know that. Maybe he could slowly run his hands down my sides, stopping on my hips and gripping them tightly in his big, strong hands. What the hell am I thinking? This is my new boss! My new boss that's hot as fuck. Stop it, Leah!* I was so in my own world I hadn't noticed that the waitress had led us to our reserved table.

Seeing Damian pull a chair out from the table, I give him a small smile and sit. I watch as he walks around to the other side and lowers in his own chair. Glancing over at me he notices I'm checking him out. Damian gives me this smouldering look and instantly I'm turned on and regretting wearing such minimal lingerie for the night.

Clearing my throat to break the tension, I grab the menu off the table and start to look it over. *Holy shit! I can't afford this! This dinner is going to take all my savings.*

Like he can read my mind, Damian speaks, "Order whatever you want, Leah. This is a business meeting after all, the company will cover it." He winks devilishly as our eyes meet. "So tell me. Did you know who I was when we met in the cafe?"

Taking a sip of my water, I look up at him and shake my head. "No, I had no idea until I walked into your office. I thought you were just some gentleman swooping in to save the lady." I smile at him.

Damian laughs, "I'm far from a gentleman, Leah. If only you knew the things I'd like to do to you right now in front of all these pompous diners."

My eyes widened at his words. "What are you suggesting, Mr Caldwell?"

Damian throws his head back and laughs, "I'm implying what you are probably thinking, Leah. I would have to be blind or ignorant not to notice how attractive you are." I go to cut him off, but he holds his hand up. "Before you say anything, you have told me this is strictly business, but it appears your body is betraying you," his fiery gaze lingers, before wandering the length of my body, a smirk bursting at the seam of his lips. He clears his throat and sits back as the waitress appears to see if we have perused the menu.

Without taking his eyes off me, Damian orders for both of us. "Two Olive Wagyu, medium-rare with vegetables, thank you." The waitress just stands there, staring at Damian. "Sorry, Was there something else you needed?" He asks politely, yet firmly.

The waitress stutters. "Ah no, sorry sir. I'll go put your order in."

Still looking at me he grins. "Now, what were we talking about? Oh, that's right, your body."

Fuck me, I'm in so much trouble. I wonder if it's too late to decline the job offer? I ponder as I rub my thighs together under the table trying to get some of the tension to release. *This is going to be a long night.*

CHAPTER 4

Damian's POV

Standing in the elevator on the way up to my office, I wonder if Leah will show up for her first day. I wouldn't be surprised if she didn't after dinner last night. Following my admission of wanting to do things to her, she started acting weird.

Stepping out onto my floor, I'm greeted by Maria. "Good morning, Sir. You have a meeting soon with the new purchasers of the Grand Hotel about the refurbishment back to the original look. They are big potential clients, Mr. Caldwell. This one is going to be exciting if we can get them." She's telling me as we walk at a fast speed towards my office.

"Maria?" I question her, she looks up at me. "Let me know when Leah shows up, please?"

I notice her smile at me and point towards the conference room door. As I walk towards my office, I peek into the meeting room to see Leah is already here setting up for the meeting... and boy does she look sexy today. Wearing a white button up shirt dress with a thick leather belt around her midsection and black lace up boots, I'm left wondering what she's got on underneath.

Like she can sense I'm staring, she stops what she's doing and looks up. "Oh, good morning Mr. Caldwell, I didn't notice you there. Maria asked me to set up for the meeting, I hope you don't mind."

Clearing my throat, "Not at all." I turn to walk to my office before stopping. "Actually, I would like you to join us for the meeting. It would be the perfect opportunity for you to understand better what the business does.Maria can sit at the desk for this one." It's taking everything I've got not to drool all over my suit every time I look at her.

Giving me a small nod she continues to put the supplies out for the meeting. I walk into my office and I close the door behind me, leaning against it before letting out the breath I hadn't realised I was holding. *What is going on here? Why does Leah make me feel like this?*

Hearing my phone ringing, I look down to see who it is. *Fucking Marisha. I can't deal with her crazy today.* Declining the call I head to my desk to get the papers ready for this morning.

Staring at the folder in front of me, my thoughts keep drifting to the beauty in the next room and that outfit she has on.

I found myself quite liking the vision my mind conjures. Her tight body, bent over the table... Those manicured fingers gripping the stained wood underneath. Her white button up dress, stretched at the seams as I rip it up, exposing that porcelain skin to the wicked sins I would deliver to her. I shuddered as I imagined those chocolate strands wrapped around my fists, her head thrown back as she gasps in guilty pleasure.

Shaking my head to get the images out of my mind, I see my office door opening slowly out of the corner of my eye. Looking over, I am greeted by Leah walking in. "Sorry to bother you Mr. Caldwell. The clients have arrived for the meeting. I have set them up in the meeting room and we are ready for you to start."

Nodding at her, "Thank you, Leah. Let's get this started, shall we?" I say, walking around from behind my desk. Standing next to Leah, I place my hand on the small of her back and I'm sure I can feel a shudder go down her spine. Guiding her into the room next to my office, I see the tables from my daydream and instantly I'm taken back there. *Get a grip, Damian. I just have to get through this meeting.*

Walking in and shaking the clients' hands I move around to the opposite side with Leah before pulling the chair out for her. I wait until she settles, before I take my own seat.

"Gentlemen, thank you for taking the time to meet with me today." I notice them both staring at Leah. "This is Leah, my new assistant, she's still learning so please excuse us if we have any side conversations, I'll just be showing her how the business operates." The men lean over to shake Leah's hand, but I notice they both hold it just a little too long and she appears uncomfortable. Clearing my throat, I put my hand gently on her leg so she knows I can tell how uncomfortable she is feeling. Looking up at me she gives me a small smile and I know she's okay.

I turn back to the men on the opposite side of the table. "Alright gentlemen, let's get this meeting underway, shall we?" I glance back at Leah, "Are you ready? When I tell you to write something down, do it. If you hear something that sounds important, make a note, okay?"

Grinning at me, "I've got it Mr. Caldwell." She starts waving her hands around. "You just do what you do and let me do my job." The sass radiating off her in waves is turning me on and making me want to tame it out of her. *You're in a meeting, Damian, get it together.* Shaking the thoughts out of my head, I got down to business.

Thirty minutes into the meeting the door flies open and Marisha comes rushing in. "Damian!" Her high pitched squeal pierces the boardroom.

All four of us jumped at the intrusion. Marisha looks between me and Leah and comes to some fucked up conclusion. "Who the fuck is *she*, Damian?" she bellows, pointing towards Leah as she races in her direction.

Standing up real quick to block her way, I catch her around her waist, stopping her from getting to Leah who's looking terrified and honestly no-one can blame her.

"Excuse us, everyone." I say with an apologetic look as I walk us out the door.

Shutting the door behind me, I turn to Marisha and glare at her. "*What* the *fuck* are you doing here, Marisha? And why are you busting into a very important meeting?" My anger is ready to explode.

She wraps herself around me, her touch feels like poison, her words like venom. "Baby, I missed you! You haven't called me."

Pulling her off me and stepping away from her. "Why would I call you when I made my intentions very clear when last we spoke? I don't want to sound like a bastard, but yesterday meant nothing. I needed to get off and you were willing." I make eye contact so she knows I mean what I'm saying. And queue the waterworks.

"I thought you loved me, Damian! We were meant to get married in a big beautiful wedding, you in a suit or whatever, me in a huge white dress looking like a princess. Why don't you love me anymore?" She stops crying and stares at me. "Damian!" *God this woman fucking scares me.*

Thankfully Maria walks in with security and they start to

drag her away, but not before she starts screaming out at me.

"Damian, you love me! Don't ever forget who was there for you when no-one else was." She turns her gaze and points at Leah, "That slut wasn't there for you, Damian, I was. I deserve more than this!" Striding towards her as security escorts her away, I stop in front of Marisha, lowering my voice to avoid further disturbance.

"You will never, and I mean *never* come to my work place again. We are not together anymore." I slow my speech to emphasize the fact. I look to security, "Don't let her in here ever again, got it?"

They nod their heads at me as they grab Marisha's arms and escort her into the elevator. I stand in front of Leah so she is out of Marisha's sight while she continues to stare daggers our way until the doors on the elevator close.

Turning around to face Leah with an apologetic look, I spoke softly "I'm so sorry about her, she's angry I broke up with her. But that was months ago and I'm pretty sure she was only with me for the money." I state matter of factly. Leah looks at me with sympathy written all over her face. Grabbing my arm, "C'mon Mr. Caldwell. Let's finish this meeting. It's too important to let that woman ruin it."

Nodding at Leah, I let her lead me back into the meeting room, shutting the door behind me as I apologise to the men about my crazy ex.

CHAPTER 5

Damian's POV

Tucked away on a street corner, walking distance from the city centre, I look up to see the unassuming terrace house. Excitement running through my veins like every time I step into this wonderland. Behind the mundane facade of the building was the interior, inky in colour and setting the mood of mystery and discretion.

Pulling the same mask I wear here every time out of my pocket, I look down to examine it. It is a piece of artwork. Representing the devil, it is painted shiny red and outlined with gold. The middle of the forehead is cut into a V making it look like horns on each side of my head and the mouthpiece has been cut out for, well, certain reasons that I am sure you can think of. Placing it on before I get inside, I think about what lies behind the door. Turning the silver door handle, I take a deep breath in before swinging the door open. I look at the grand entrance and it feels like home. I head towards the bar that is in a side room from the entrance. As I walk through the doors, I see the bodies that are entwined together along the sidelines. The touching, the grinding, the moans, the pleasure that is happening around me makes the excitement that much more.

Pulling up one of the black stools at the bar, I sit and watch, waiting, looking for the one I came here to meet.

Victoria, the seductress who is my sub. The waist-length blonde curls are the first thing I notice as she comes through the doors of the bar, wearing the mask I bought her. The black lace shaped over the top half of her face making the red lipstick covering her luscious lips stand out. Lipstick that surely will be smudged by the end of our session. As she walks closer to where I am I notice the outfit she wears. The black lace of the bodice flowing over her remarkable breasts and chest as the straps sit on top of her perky tits, flowing from the valley between them. Black lace sitting over her toned stomach but still showing enough skin to see the abs she has as the straps dangle down and attach to her sexy black pantyhose. That's when I notice the very small, barely there, black lace G-string she is wearing and topping off the outfit with red pumps. Licking my lips as she finally gets to me, she knows exactly what is about to happen. Grabbing her by the throat I pull her to me, our lips clashing. The kiss is sloppy and needy. Something I need after all the sexual tension with Leah today at the office.

Using my free hand, I wrap it around her body, trailing down her spine slowly until I finally make it to the top of her ass. That round, chunky and incredibly sexy ass. Fanning my giant hand over one of her ass cheeks, I squeeze it hard, making her groan and catching it in my mouth, silencing her noises.

Pulling her off my lips, I grin at her. "We are in room five. Go get yourself ready for me." I watch as she turns to go, grabbing her around the waist and pulling her back into my chest. I slowly lean down to her ear, moving her hair out of the way and whisper, "Get ready baby girl, I have some energy to burn off today." I hear her let out a small moan and know my words are making her drip down her legs.

Watching her as she walks away, I think about all the toys I plan to use on her tonight. I turn and sit back down on my stool at the bar, and throw back the whiskey the bartender got for me while I was occupied with Victoria. The best thing about being well known in this community is when I need a new sub, I always have many females willing to see if we gel as a dynamic. They all know that I am respectful and loyal. Boundaries are set in place on both sides and are always abided by and my aftercare is something to be desired. I know some other Dominants who are amazing Doms and their aftercare is sought after, but it still isn't the same level as mine.

Sliding off the stool, I start heading out of the bar doors, taking a right before walking down the long black-walled hallway. The doors I pass are closed, the sexy mysteries that are behind them exciting me. I stop outside the door that is closed with the number five on it. This is my room. This is the room I always get. I knock on the door letting Victoria know I'm here so she can get into position. Placing my hand on the silver door handle, I turn it and push open the door.

My eyes scan the room, taking in the black coloured walls and stopping at the woman with blonde hair who stands at the end of the bed wearing nothing but the black, barely there lace bodice and red pumps.

Closing the door, I take my jacket off and throw it over the back of a chair as I walk towards Victoria, stopping in front of her. Pointing to the timber head of the bed, I say with force. "Sit down, there. You do not speak. You wait." She grins as she says, "Yes Daddy." She knows what is to come as she takes her place on the bed. I climb up onto the bed. Starting at her feet and slowly making my way up her body, straddling her as I get to her chest. Grabbing her under the arms, I push them up gently, making sure her hands reach the head of the bed. Bending down, I lick up her neck, working to her ear, nipping the skin on the way. Stopping below her ear, I nip the sensitive skin... hard. It takes everything in Victoria not to make a sound. I can see the struggle on her face. For a brief moment I see something in Victoria that reminds me of Leah. Blinking hard and shaking my head, getting the images of Leah out of my mind as I continue my assault on Victoria's neck and ear.

Sitting up, still straddling her, I slowly slide my leg over her chest as I reach for the ties I had set up earlier for us.

As I bind her arms to the bed, I think about what I plan to do to her. The ropes, the toys, the pain, and she will love it all. It's one of the reasons Victoria is a great sub. The trust she has in me is impeccable. We know each other so well that I know when I push her to her boundaries, even if she doesn't say her safe words. The thought has me wondering what will happen when she finds herself a man. I shake the thought off so I can be in the here, in the now as I slide off the side of the bed, reaching for the tie that is still wrapped around my neck. Turning to face Victoria I pull the tie from around my neck, the action fast and full of desire.

She watches as I undo the buttons on my shirt, one by one, not making a sound. There's a knock on the door and I turn my head towards the sound as a small voice follows.

"Ahh, excuse me? Um. Sorry to interrupt but I need to speak with you, Sir. It is rather important."

I look back down to my submissive tied to the bed, pointing to her. "YOU! Do. Not. Make. A. Sound. I will be back."

As I walk to the door my shirt flaps open showing my large chest and the tattoo's scattered all over the canvas. Swinging the door open, I see the waitress waiting patiently, just staring at my pants. Looking down I grin at my semi hard cock that was starting to tent my pants. I clear my throat to get her attention to shift to my face. "Can I help you? Are you ok?" Her fiery red hair makes her skin seem paler then it probably is and making the blush that shows on her cheeks stand out even more. "Miss?" I say trying to get her attention. Gathering herself she stands up straight, but would still stand a whole foot shorter than myself.

"Um, Sir. The boss wanted to come down and let you know that someone told the paparazzi you are here again and they are trying to get in. We have organised a helicopter to come get you and take you to the closest airport where we have a car waiting to take you home."

I just stand there. "You have a leak in your staff. This has happened too many times to be a coincidence. Tell your boss she needs to sort it. Now, I'm going to go back to my sub and get her organised. Leave us." I turn my back on the woman before she even gets a chance to respond, closing the door behind me. Leaning my back on the door, I exhale. *Who the fuck keeps telling the paps where I am?*

CHAPTER 6

Leah's POV

I have been sitting at my desk for the last two hours waiting for Damian to walk through the door, but he still isn't here. It's 10am. *Where the hell could he be?* He is normally the first one here and now I wonder if I should start to worry. I stood up to go over to Maria's desk to ask if he had an early meeting I wasn't aware of when he stumbled out the elevator doors wearing yesterday's suit and looking like shit. I start to run up to him to see if he is okay, when Marisha, the ex, steps out from behind him with a slimy grin on her face. I stop dead in my tracks. *What the fuck is she doing here?*

Slowly making my way towards Damian I watch as Marisha steps in front of him, crosses her arms and sticks one of her legs out to the side of the long black cocktail dress, the slit going so high you can see she isn't wearing any underwear.

"Mr. Caldwell? Are you okay? What happened last night? You look awful." I look at Marisha who's still grinning from ear to ear. The kind of grin that makes you want to cut a bitch.

Marisha speaks up, breaking the silence. "He's fine. You act like he's been up to no good, he's been with me..." She pauses. Turning herself around and wrapping her arms around Damian's neck, pulling him down, crashing their lips together. She pulls away from him, "c'mon baby, let's go to your office." She grabs his hand, dragging him along the hallway towards his office when Maria jumps in front of her. Marisha stops dead in her tracks, towering over the older lady, but seemingly intimidated by the aged beauty. "Marisha, You know good and well that the only way you can get Mr. Caldwell now is when he is drunk. You've had your fun for the night, now leave." She waves Marisha off. Marisha doesn't move, just stares down at Maria with disgust written all over her face. I watch as Maria's face turns red. *Oh shit, is she about to have a heart attack?* I watch as Maria stands up next to Marisha, her head held high as she calmly but firmly says, "I SAID LEAVE, MARISHA!"

As Marisha stands still, I can't help but look between the women. *I wonder what happened between Marisha and Damian?*

I get pulled from my thoughts by a loud slap. I look in the direction the sound came from and see Marisha standing there, hand over her mouth as Maria holds the side of her face, her eyes open wide with surprise and some of her grey hair has been moved from her bun from the force of the slap. Damian stares between the two women, not understanding what's happening. As I walk over to him, I see Maria start to step back and security walk up behind Marisha grabbing her arms and pulling her away, escorting her to the elevator as she screams out obscenities at the men.

Grabbing Damian's arm, I started to walk him to his office. I stop at the heavy wooden door and grab the handle, turning it slightly so we can enter. Just as I push the door open, Damian vomits all over the black carpet in front of him. I jump back, avoiding wearing any of the splash back, squealing as I do. Drawing Damian's attention to me, he looks at me apologetically.

"Leah? What are you doing here? How did you know about the party?" Damian slurs through the sentence. "How much have you had to drink, Sir?" He grins at me and if he didn't have vomit dripping down his chin my panties would have a wet spot. He slurs to me, "Sir, huh?" Raising an eyebrow at me. Even though he is absolutely wasted, he is still a smooth motherfucker. Full of confidence and oozing of sex appeal. I start to giggle at him. "Come on Mr. Caldwell, Let's get you on the couch." Before I could even think of my next words, Damian leans down to my ear and whispers, "only if you are going to join me, Leah." And with just those few words this man has made me ruin another pair of panties, even with vomit breath.

Inhaling deep into my lungs, I hold it. This man is making my new job hard to do. Letting out the breath. "I don't think so, Mr. Caldwell. You need to sleep it off." Guiding him to the black leather couch, I push him down so he is sitting. He looks up at me, raising one of his eyebrows. His voice was hoarse and full of desire. "Leah? You are beautiful, you know that?" I stop in the position I'm in as my eyes grow wide. Damian lifts his big hands and uses the back of them to slide up the inside of my bare legs, stopping before he gets to the one place I want him to touch. My breathing stops with anticipation, but he makes no move. I brave looking down at his face to see he had fallen asleep. *Are you fucking serious?*

As I remove his hands from the inside of my legs I see Maria come through the door. "Need some help, love? He's a big man, you won't be able to move him yourself." We both giggle as we slide his back down the couch.

Walking around and grabbing his shoulders I pull him up so his head is using the arm rest as a pillow. We both walk around the couch, meeting in the middle. Maria speaks first. "You know, he really is a good man. A good man with a crazy past. Once he grew up and pulled himself together, he started to let the good man he is shine through the bullshit. Remember that, okay?" She walks out of the office, leaving me standing there staring at this beautiful man. I know he is a good person, he stood up for me. A random woman in a cafe. A nobody, and he stood up to that man. In that moment, he made me feel like I could matter... I could be someone.

As I undo his shoe laces and slide off his fancy italian leather shoes, I notice he is wearing odd socks, making me giggle. Shaking my head, I pull the small throw from the back of the couch over Damian.

Heading to the door, I stop in front of it and turn around, taking in one more glance at the handsome sleeping man.

CHAPTER 7

Damian's POV

Groaning as I come to, I have to wonder, what the fuck happened last night. The first thing I notice as my eyes flutter open is the black coffee table to the side of me with a bottle of water and a pack of panadol on it. *Hang on, I don't have a coffee table in my bedroom.* I slowly look around the room I'm in. It's dark, there are no lights on and the blinds are closed. *Am I in my office? How did I even get here?* When I try to sit up I get light headed. I see my phone sitting on the floor next to me. Laying myself back down, I slap my hand around the spot my phone should be, hoping I get it. After a few minutes that felt like a few years, I opened it up and searched for Leah's number. Scrolling through my contacts until I finally find it, my thumb hovering over the little green call button. *Stop stalling, man, just call her to come into your office.* Hitting the call button, I hear her mobile ring just outside the door and the small voice that comes through the speaker. "Sir?" I pause, flashes of Leah calling me Sir and me asking her to join me on the seat go through my mind. "Mr. Caldwell? That's it, I'm coming in." I can hear the panic in her voice as she speaks. Hanging up as she runs through the doorway, coming to a sudden halt in front of me. Kneeling on the floor in front of me, she whispers. "Damian? Are you ok? Have you had anything for the hangover?" I can't help but look at this woman. Like really look at her. She's beautiful. She's the type of woman you take home to meet mum. And it's not just her beauty that's striking. You can tell what kind of person she is, it shines through her skin like a constant glow. Her soul is kind and way out of my league. I can't want her, I can't bring her into this life. The life I'm forced to live is hard and public. She is too gentle to survive it.

Snapping fingers in front of my face brings me to the now. I look up to see Leah, concern written all over her face. Man, do I look that bad? I probably do. I mean, I feel like I've been hit by a truck... over and over and over again. Going by the thumping going on in my head, the truck is reversing as well. "Damian? What is going on in that head?"

Clearing my throat, I answer her. "Stop. Stop yelling at me... Please." Throwing my arm over my eyes, I sigh as I hear her sit down. "Please, Leah. Just leave me." She starts laughing, loud. "Well, I would love to, but the work day has just started and you have been asleep on this couch for 24 hours. Here's an idea. I'll take you home. While you have a shower, I will make you a great hangover feast, how about that?"

I shift my arm up my face slightly so I can see her face and instantly I can tell she is serious. "What? You want to take me home and cook for me?" I question, raising my eyebrow at her. She is still smiling at me when I put my arm over my head. I watch as the smile leaves her face. "Okay Casanova. You stink. Let's get you home and you can shower." She stands, holding her hand out for me to take. "C'mon, Damian. I wasn't joking. You have been asleep in here since yesterday morning and you need a shower. So come on. I'll take you home." Her hand hangs between us as I sigh. "You know I'm *your* boss, right? I should be bossing you around. But I will never say no to being cooked food by a beautiful woman, even one that keeps turning me down."

I hear giggles as I sit up and look at Leah. She's standing in front of me in her skin tight navy dress. Its long sleeves and a high neckline covering her top half as her bare legs show under the short bottom half. I can imagine her spreading her legs and mounting me right here on this couch as I slide her panties to the side and undo my zipper as my rock solid cock finds her entrance.

"Ahhhh, Mr. Caldwell?" I hear Leah say. She's still in front of me. She is pointing to my pants and as I look down I realise I have a raging boner. *Well this was an unexpected turn of events.* Standing up I stride into the ensuite and close the door behind me, not wanting to show her how embarrassed I really was. "Just give me a minute, okay Leah? I'll meet you at your desk." I hold my breath, waiting to hear her response but all I hear is the office door being closed.

As I unzip my pants and pull my dick out, slowly stroking it from base to tip, going back into the scenario I have already started imagining with Leah straddling me on the couch, I start moving my hand a little faster as I imagine slipping my cock into Leah's tight pussy. Groaning at the thought, I start pumping myself harder and faster, imagining Leah as she bounces on my dick, fucking me like I've never been fucked before. Imagining her as she moans with pleasure. Looking at myself in the mirror as I finally come, grunting as I spray myself all over the sink I had been holding onto. As I tuck myself back into my pants I grab the hand towel, wiping the sink down to destroy any evidence of what happened. Looking into the mirror once more before turning and walking out the door so that the woman I just wanked over can take me home. *Well, this is going to be something.*

CHAPTER 8

Leah's POV

As I follow Damian's directions, weaving through the traffic and going down back streets, I notice we are getting further away from the "fancy" part of the city and heading more to the suburbs. Looking around, I question him. "Are you sure we are going the right way?" Damian whips his head around, looking at me.

"Yeah, Leah. I know where I live." The eye roll he didn't do was implied. He scoffs at me as he points at a house to the right. "There. That's mine."

I pull into the driveway and stop at the garage, my eyes not leaving the two story modest house. It's not at all what I was expecting. I was expecting some penthouse bachelor pad, not the white picket fence he lives in. I sit in the driver's seat looking over at the house, taking in the white cladding that wraps around it and the white shutters on all the windows. The swinging seat that sits on the front veranda rocks slightly with the breeze that is going past it. Stepping out of the car, I look around the beautiful property before moving towards the front door where Damian is waiting for me. Walking up the five little steps onto the front porch, I can see the copious amounts of pot plants that are lining the railings. The aqua door stood out from all the white that surrounds it. Damian grunts as he unlocks and opens the coloured door, stepping to the side allowing me to walk through.

As I step inside the humble home, I look around the small hallway. The light grey walls are bare of photos or art. I can't help myself and start walking forward, investigating further into the house. Stopping at the bottom of the staircase I turn and look at Damian who is eyeing me and my next moves.

"Mr. Caldwell. You should go have a shower. Just point me to the kitchen and I'll see what I can whip up for you." He gives me a smirk that makes my panties want to drop. Damian steps closer to me, leaning down to my ear and says in a low growl, "I'll show you, Leah." The sound of his voice making a wet spot form on my panties. All I can do is nod at him. I don't trust myself to open my mouth, I can feel the moan in my throat wanting to leave. Even though there is plenty of room around us, Damian brushes his chest against mine as he tries to go around me, making me suck in a breath and hold it. The stale smell of him mixed with his cologne still lingering as he walks away through the lounge room and into a back room. Following him, I walk into a beautiful old style kitchen but with modern perks. Nothing fancy, just updated. Walking up to the fridge, I open it and bend over, looking at what food he has for me to cook for him. Without looking from the inside of the fridge, I say. "Okay, you can go shower now. I've got it from here. I'll organise some food for you." Suddenly, it feels like he is right behind me. I can feel him. He's not touching me but I can feel his presence. My heart is pounding in my chest so loud I swear he can hear it, but all he does is walk away towards his bathroom.

Finally being able to relax, I look around the fridge, finding the things to make Damian some bacon and eggs. Collecting everything needed to make the breakfast, I slam the fridge door shut with my foot as I walk away. As I head over to the island benchtop, I spot the stainless steel gas stovetop and it's absolutely beautiful. Carefully, I unload the food next to it as I stare. I've never seen something so beautiful in my life. To say I grew up poor is an understatement. My parents kicked me out at the age of twelve and I lived on the streets until I ran into a lovely woman that moved me in with her. Did we struggle? Yes, we did. Did she love me? Like I was her own. Am I eternally grateful for everything she gave me? Always. I wouldn't be here if she hadn't taken me in. Hearing the pan sizzling, I noticed I had been so wrapped up in my thoughts I didn't notice that I had already put the bacon in the pan and it was crispy and ready to be eaten. Finding a spare dish, I put the cooked bacon in it and place it next to the stove as I start frying the eggs. I spy a hand sneaking past me and take some bacon. I turn around and my jaw drops to the floor. Standing in front of me is Damian. Soaking wet from the shower in nothing but a towel hanging low on his hips. Honestly not much is left to my imagination, I can see what he is packing underneath. He stands there in front of me, smirking as I watch the water drip from his dark hair and down his chest, over his abs, getting caught by the top of the towel, and it takes all my willpower not to walk up to him and run my finger tips over his naked chest, following the path the droplets have taken. Without taking his gorgeous green eyes away from my own he steps forward, he moves so that he is now directly in front of me, making me crane my head up to see his face. I knew he was tall and muscular, but right now? With the way we are standing? I felt so, so tiny. His huge body engulfed me as he towered above me. The need to touch him comes back but this time I can't resist it. I stare at his shoulders and run my fingertips down his body. Going over the muscles that he works so hard for and stopping at the towel, I contemplate if I want him to drop the towel but unfortunately, I don't get to make that choice. The room fills with smoke and the smoke alarm gets activated. Fucking great. Damian jumps into action, throwing me out of the way, grabbing the pan, throwing it in the sink and turning on the water. Instantly it stops smoking as Damian turns to me. My hand is covering my mouth and I look between the man standing before me and the steaming pan. "I am so sorry, Mr. Caldwell. Oh my god. I nearly burned your house down." I start to pace as Damian laughs at me, walking to me and grabbing my shoulders, stopping me from moving. "You hardly nearly burned down my house. Burnt the eggs, but not the house." He laughs at me. How could I tell him I burned the eggs because I couldn't take my eyes (and hands) off him?

CHAPTER 9

Damian's POV

Standing in the shower washing the last 24 hours off, I can't help but let my mind wander to Leah downstairs in my kitchen cooking for me. How sexy she would look running around making me something to eat. The thought of her down there making sure I am being looked after makes me hard. Why is this tiny woman having this effect on me? Standing under the spray, I let my hand slowly run down my abs, palming my semi-hard dick. Groaning at the touch, I imagine my hand is Leah's mouth gliding up and down my cock, giving me the pleasure I imagine her beautiful mouth could give. I stop moving for a moment, using my imagination to help me with my fantasy. Placing my free hand on the white tiles of the shower wall, I close my eyes and grab my dick again. Using my hand, I imagine I have Leah pushed hard against the wall as I slide myself into her and grab her around the throat, gently squeezing. I start off moving slowly, making every movement count. I can feel myself slide in and out of her, the feeling of her pussy tight around me. I start stroking myself a little faster, imagining Leah bent over in front of me, allowing me to thrust myself into her while she shows me her asshole. I bet she's never been fucked in the ass. The thought turns me on even more, bringing me closer to the edge - one

I'd happily fall over for a small taste of that woman. I can't help the small, deep growl that leaves my mouth as I spray cum all over the shower wall. It is the most intense orgasm I've ever given myself.

Placing my other hand on the wall, I hold myself up as I slow down my breathing. We don't want Leah to know what I was doing up here. Spraying the cum on the wall as it runs down, cleaning the spot. I also soap myself up. After washing myself I step out, grabbing the fluffy towel and wrapping it low around my waist. I may just have to see what Leah will do if I walk downstairs in just my towel.

Opening the bathroom door, I head towards the kitchen where I can hear all the noise. I stand in the kitchen doorway watching Leah cooking. As I sneak up behind her, I can smell her and she smells like heaven. I stand there, watching, taking notes. She is tiny, about five foot two. Her chocolate coloured hair is half up, the back half is down and begging to be moved to the side so I can grab her by the throat and run kisses down her neck. Shaking my head, I pull myself from the fantasy. I'm standing right behind her now as she moves the bacon to a fresh plate and cracks eggs into the hot pan. I reach around her grabbing a piece of the crunchy bacon and stepping back. I stand there in front of her, smirking as she watches the water drip from my dark hair and down my chest, over my abs, getting caught by the top of the towel I have wrapped around my waist. Without taking my eyes away from her own, I step forward. I am now directly in front of Leah and I watch as she cranes her head to look at my face. She is so tiny standing next to me as my huge body engulfed her. I stand still, staring into Leah's eyes. She looks like she wants to do something so I stay still. She finally makes a move as she places her hands on my shoulders and runs her fingers down my body. Tracing over the muscles that I work so hard for and stopping at the top of the towel, I pray she pulls it apart so it falls. I desperately want to have her but I don't get to make that choice. The room fills with smoke and the smoke alarm gets activated. Fucking great, I jump into action. Throwing Leah out of the way of any danger, I grab the pan and throw it in the sink, turning on the water. Instantly it stops smoking and I turn around to Leah. She looks in shock, her hand is covering her mouth and she glances between me and the steaming pan. "I am so sorry, Mr Caldwell. Oh my God. I nearly burned your house down," Leah says as she starts to pace. Laughing at her, I walked to her and grabbed her shoulders so I could stop her from moving. "You hardly nearly burned down my house. Burnt the eggs, but not the house." I laughed harder at her.

The ice has been broken and the adrenaline is running through us. I bend down, crashing my lips to hers. I feel her resist so I start to back away but before our lips come apart I feel her pull me back down. It is at this moment I realised I wouldn't be able to stop myself from having her even if I wanted to. Running my hands down her spine, I come to a stop on her ass. Spreading my hands out over her cheeks, I grab them and squeeze, earning myself a moan from her, the sound egging me on in my adventure of this amazing woman's body. Picking her up by her ass cheeks, I move us over to the island bench and place her down as I move myself to stand between her legs. Grabbing her face in both my hands as we move our mouths against each other, I can't help but make a low growl. I pull away from her mouth, resting my forehead on hers and whispering, "We shouldn't do this, Leah." I exhale, close my eyes and continue. "But I don't know if I can stop, or if I even want to stop." I feel hands on my face and I open my eyes to see Leah looking into my soul. Without any thought I lean into her lips, gently kissing her. It is different than I have ever kissed before. It's normally frantic and rushed. This is needier and filled with passion. Like if we don't kiss, the world will end. I start kissing my way over her jaw to her ear, biting it gently. Moving on to her neck as I lick and kiss my way down to her collarbone. Her phone starts ringing, breaking us apart. Both of us were breathless from the makeout session. Leah looks at her phone then back to me. "I need to get that, it could be work." She grins at me as she answers. Okay, girlie. I see how you roll. We playing like that huh?

CHAPTER 10

Damian's POV

It's been a week since Leah and I kissed in my kitchen. I need to talk to her about it, we need to clear the air. The tension in the office is insane and people are starting to ask questions. To say the talk around the watercooler was explosive is an understatement. The office gossip has us all but married. Actually, it's the end of the week, they most likely have us married and divorced. Nothing gets past them.

"Helllooooo? Damian? You there buddy?" I look up to see Markus standing in front of me clicking his fingers. Markus, my best mate. The one person who I trust with my life. The only person I will openly say is a handsome mother fucker. He is the only person who can pull me up on my shit and I listen. Mainly because he is the only one who can physically beat the shit out of me and the only one who can get away with it.

As I drop my forehead onto the table I inhale slowly before letting it out in a groan.

"Markus. I don't know what the fuck you are talking about. Honestly, I'm not listening. I can't stop thinking about the...." I stumble on my words. I haven't mentioned what happened to anyone, including Markus. I lift my head off the table slowly to see him sitting in the chair on the other side, his big arms folded across his chest and a dirty smirk on his face.

"I know what you did with Marisha the other week, you dirty dog." He shakes his head at me. I groan and lower my head back onto the table as I remember what we did right here in this office. How I fucked her mouth and how she had let me. Mumbling to him without lifting my head, "It wasn't my finest moment, that's for sure." I look back up to my best friend, seeing the pain on his face. He knows what I went through to get her to somewhat leave me after the breakup. Now I have fucked that up. "Man, she's always coming around here, storming into my office, acting like we are together. Just last week I had her thrown out of here by security." I throw my hands in the air as I slide the chair out from under me with my legs, knocking it over. "It's just. You know what she is like. She is a psycho." Walking around my desk now with my hands on my hips and shaking my head before sitting next to Markus. "Man, I have fucked up, haven't I?" Watching my best mate as he pats me on the shoulder and nods. "Yeah, mate. You fucked up real good this time. You know what she's like. She is a level one clinger. Remember what she was like? Do you remember the shit she put you through? I do, mate. I do. Because I was there to help you pick up the pieces of your life after she destroyed it." He sighs as he runs his fingers through his dark hair and looks at me with those eyes that look into your soul.

"I know. I know." The defeat was evident in my tone.

A gentle knock on the closed office door brought both our heads around. "Yeah, come in." I watch the door slowly open to reveal Leah and I look towards Markus. His eyes widen and I know where his head is. He wants her and the thought of her with anyone else other than me makes my blood boil.

"Ah, sorry Mr. Caldwell. I didn't realise you were busy. I was just coming to see if there is anything else you need me to do before I finish up for the day?" Leah looks at Markus and blushes, like looking at him is turning her on and that fucker knows what he is doing.I dont think you need this, just she blushed and then Markus raises eyebrow I watch as he raises an eyebrow at her before standing. Walking up to her, he puts his hand out, hoping to shake her hand. "Hi. Since this guy isn't going to introduce us…" he turns and stares at me and continues, "…which is very rude, I must say." Turning to look back at Leah. "I am Markus. Apparently he and I are best friends. He told me he had a new PA, but he seemed to skip telling me how beautiful she is." Turning back to me. "Shame on you, Damian. Shame on you." He goes to turn his attention back to Leah but to find her attention is on me, as she walks towards me to find she is walking towards me.

Looking at me with those big innocent eyes, "Mr. Caldwell? Did you need anything else? I just need to let my housemate know when to pick me up, is all." I smile at her weakly.

"No, Leah. That is all for today. Are you still okay to come in tomorrow for a few hours for us to go over the contracts for the Mitchell accounts?" Leah smiles and nods. "Excellent. Say around 10.30? Do you need a car to pick you up or can you get here?" Leah laughs at me. "It's fine, my housemate can drop me off." Her phone dings and she looks down at it. "And speak of the devil. The devil is waiting at my desk. Night Mr. Caldwell." She goes to walk off towards the door as I jump up and stride to her. Opening the door for her and following her out. I stop and see some random guy standing in the hallway.

His face lights up when he sees Leah. She walks up to him and wraps her arms around him. I can't help but stare him down. He is tall, especially standing next to her. His blonde surfer guy hair looking like it was washed by the ocean and his blue eyes throwing daggers towards me as he runs his hands up and down her back. She lets him go and turns around. "Oh god, how rude of me. Mr. Caldwell, this is my housemate, Mike. Mike, this is my boss, Mr. Caldwell." I reach my hand out to greet him but all he does is stare at it. Okay then, that wasn't very nice was it? This totally feels like it needs a mind your manners in there, but just me being silly maybe Leah turns back towards her 'housemate' "Cmon Mike, I'm starving. You need to feed me before we get home." Turning and waving at me as she walks off, all I can think about is how much her housemate is a fucking douche and how much I would love to take him down a peg or two.

CHAPTER 11

Damian's POV

I am already knee deep in paperwork by the time Leah shows up for work. I watch her as she walks between the open desks of the other staff members. She greets them all by name, stopping to chat to some of them. I watch her as she talks. Gesturing with her hands as she talks, the corner of her mouth turning up to form a lopsided smile. I notice it doesn't reach her eyes, it's not a real smile. Something is wrong with her, she is off. I wonder what is going on. I wonder if it has anything to do with that housemate, I roll my eyes as I think about him. There's something about him that makes my skin crawl. I will find out what he is about. Sooner or later I will find something. Maybe just Sooner or later I will find out what he is all about, or what his deal is

I notice Leah walking towards her desk to get herself settled in, waving at me as she does. I lift my hand to wave back,when I see her pulling her sleeve down on her right arm. She winces like she is in pain. I will have to pull her aside and ask her in private if she is okay.

I let her settle in before I get up and walk out to her.

"Morning Leah. How was your evening after you clocked off last night? Did you manage to go eat?" I clear my throat, not really caring about the food she ate. I just want to know if her 'roommate' is more than her roommate.

"Oh, hi Mr Caldwell." She giggles and I can tell her heart is not in it. "Um, no. We didn't get to stop for food. Mike needed to get home and since he didn't let me take the bus I didn't want to nag him." She shrugs like it wasn't a big deal. As I nod, pretending that I'm not thinking of ways to hurt this guy, she keeps talking, but I honestly can't concentrate on anything. "Ah, Damian?" Leah whispers in front of my face, breaking me from my thoughts. Shaking my head and answering her. "Yeah? Sorry, got lost in my head there for a sec. What do you need?" She stands up and I watch her pencil skirt slide back down her porcelain thighs. Touching the same skin I have imagined gliding my own hands up and making her call me Daddy as she grabs handfuls of my hair and guides me to the one place she wants, no, NEEDS me to be. Pulling my head between her legs, letting me taste her sweetness right here at her desk. A hand wraps around my arm and I feel myself getting pulled away and out of my head at the same time. Pulling me away from my daydream is Leah, striding towards my office looking cranky. She slams the door open so hard she nearly shatters the glass walls that are my office. Everyone stops what they are doing and looks at us as she drags me through it and slams it behind me. Why!? What happened? Got smidge lost here, unless intentional that we too are lost in Damian's head and confused.

Leah turns and looks at me, the look on her face telling me exactly what mood she is in. She storms her way up to me so we are chest to chest, or more like her chest my waist. Poking her finger into my pec she whisper-yells, "Stop! Stop it, Damian." Confusion written all over my face. "Stop what, Ms Williams?" her name rolling off my tongue like it is the one word I am meant to speak for the rest of my life. "Stop that, Mr Caldwell. Stop the way you are looking at me." She is starting to get frantic, talking fast and pacing in front of me. I can tell she is nervous, but why? I mean, she couldn't know what I was thinking about before... Could she? I stop her, grabbing both her biceps and she inhales, like she is in pain. Leah looks up at me, her eyes wide open in shock, like I have just discovered her big secret. I let go of her and watch as she looks through the office windows to all the staff who are still watching us. I see how upset Leah is now, so making the decision I close the blinds in my office. I sit Leah on the couch as I sit down next to her. "What is going on? Leah?" Looking up at me with sad eyes she just shakes her head. Stumbling over her words, she tries to talk, not looking me in the eyes. "I... Um.... I.... Can't say it." I don't want to push it but I feel like this, whatever this is, is serious and she needs help. I go to grab her hand and for the first time I notice the red marks around her wrists. I slide her sleeve up a little and she goes still, kind of. She starts shaking, whole body shakes. I try to keep my tone even, but it's hard when your mind is racing with scenarios of why she has these marks. "Leah? Why do you have these marks?" I look at her, pleading with her. "Leah. Please. Tell me. Why do you have these marks? If it was consensual then say so and you can be on your way, but if this is something you didn't want and someone did it to you anyway? Well, I can't make any promises there." Tears start falling down Leah's cheeks as she falls into my body pulling me in as tight as she could, needing to feel the protection I obviously make her feel.

Feeling her sob uncontrollably, her whole body shakes with the emotions, I lay her head in my lap, getting her comfortable. Just letting her do what she needs to do, letting her get it out. We are in silence, the only sound is the sound of her crying. I hope she has someone in her life she can trust with whatever is going on, but I'm going to make sure she knows she can trust me. I need to help this woman.

CHAPTER 12

Leah's Pov

I stare out the window as we move through the streets of the city in Mike's souped up Nissan GTR. The matte grey exterior makes the black and grey interior stand out and with good cause, this car is sexy and I always feel sexy driving in it. I watch as the buildings pass us by while I ponder life. God I love it here. I am anonymous. I am a nobody and that is exactly how I like it. I have a couple of friends that I trust with my life and couldn't imagine my life without those two women. As much as I love them and trust them, they have no idea what has been going on for the past few months. Nobody knows and I need to keep it that way. I don't want anyone to get hurt because of me, because of my choices.

"So, do you like your new job? Seems like a nice group of people." Mike says as he puts his hand on my knee. I stare where he is touching me, hoping he doesn't go any higher. I knew I should have worn pants today, a skirt makes it far too easy for him. I can't help but squeeze my eyes closed. If I can't see it, it's not happening, right?

"Leah? I asked you a question. Are you planning on answering me?" His words were harsh and demanding as he squeezed my thigh trying to get my attention back on him. Opening my eyes, I glance over at him. "Um, yeah. They are really nice and I am learning so much from Mr. Caldwell. I think I may like to do this as a career." I shrug like it's no big deal, just a thought. "But you would find somewhere else to work, right?" I knew it, I knew as soon as I mentioned Damian, Mike would arch up at me. Feeling the car come to an abrupt stop I notice we are out the front of my office building. I remove his hand from my leg and open the door, sliding out onto the pavement. Taking a deep breath I turn and face the car, closing the door before stepping back and into a hard chest, apologising. "I am so sorry. I didn't mean to run into you." An arm wraps around my waist as I turn to see who it was. It's Mike and he is leaning down as if he is going to kiss me. If I turn my head to avoid it he will cause a scene and that is the last thing I need right now. I stand on my tippy toes, meeting his lips with my own. He wraps his free arm around my waist and squeezes me tight as he pulls my feet off the ground. I let him do as he wanted and made it look like I was enjoying myself. Mike groans into my mouth as we kiss. The thought of his lips on mine makes me feel sick as he slowly pulls his face away from me. Dropping me to the ground like a sack of potatoes, Mike gives me his creepy side grin. "Mmm, baby. That was amazing and I nearly believed you wanted it." He says, running the pads of his thumb across my lip, wiping his spit from it. "I will pick you up when you finish work, I will have a surprise waiting for you, you are going to love it." His slimy grin lets me know I'm not actually going to love it.

Pulling away from him, I nod and speak quietly. "Okay Mike. I will be ready." Mike grabbed my arm as I tried to walk away, running the back of his hand down the side of my face. "You are such a good girl, Leah. Who's my good girl?" I will do anything to get out of this situation. It makes me sick to my stomach, this hold he has on me. If I didn't believe he would hurt the people I loved then I would have left already, but this man is unpredictable. I never know what to expect from him. "Huh, Leah? Are you my good girl?" I looked up at his face. "Always, Mike. I am always your good girl." I spy the entrance of the building. "I have to get in the office now, I don't want to be late. I will see you tonight." I rush off to the doors, gliding in through them and breathing a sigh of relief that I have all day without the worry of my housemate.

Damian's POV

Going to get coffee for the 3 of us was the best idea I think I've ever had. Stepping out of the doorway of the little cafe, I see a grey car pull up across the road in front of the offices. It's the kind of car I see douchebags drive thinking they are something special and treating their women like shit. As I walk across the road I glance back at the douche car and notice Leah step out. She doesn't notice when Mike gets out of the car and stands right behind her, watching me watch them. I see him give me a sly grin as he turns his attention back to Leah. She is deep in thought when she turns, closes the door and steps backwards, running into her housemate. I watch as he wraps his arm around her and Leah turns around speaking as she does. Mike leans down as I see Leah meet him halfway, their lips colliding in a passionate kiss and I know the show is for me, I know he is showing me who she belongs to. Spying them kissing is making me angry, the jealousy burning through my veins wishing it was me she was embracing, not *him*. Wondering why she would tell me he's only a housemate has me distracted to the point I didn't notice that Leah had left and Mike was standing in front of me with his arms hanging down his sides, his fists clenched and a scowl on his face.

"Oh, hey Mike!" Pretending I actually care that he is standing in front of me. "How have you been? Just dropping Leah off?"

He takes a step, inching closer to me until we are almost chest to chest. Getting in my face while poking me in the pec with his finger as he says in a lowly voice. "Leah. Is. MINE! She has been MINE for a long time and she will be MINE for even longer." I look at him, confused. "I thought you guys were roommates?" I ask him.

Scoffing at me he glares at me in my eyes, "Oh mate, we are so much more than roommates. I know how good her sweet tight pussy feels wrapped around my cock." Grinning at me as he says the last few words. "I know how you feel about her, your body language gives you away, mate. But like I said, she's mine and only mine." He is smug, like he has won a prize that the other kid wanted and as much as I would love to knock him out, I calmly reply. "Oh yeah? Is that why she couldn't take her hands off me last week when she took me home and helped me out?" I wink at him as I sidestep around his big frame and walk towards the front of the office building. Before opening the doors I turn to look at him one more time to find him speeding off up the road. I wonder why Leah told me they were roommates and not together?

CHAPTER 13

Leah's POV

Sitting down on my office seat, I work hard to keep the shaking to a minimum until I've hidden behind my desk. My ass hits the chair just as my legs give out. I desperately want to burst out crying but also don't want to give Mike the satisfaction of getting the better of me. He gets enough out of me and I refuse to let him take any more. The ding from the elevator brings my attention to it. The door opens, exposing a furious looking Damian, who storms down the walkway through the office. The office grows quiet as he passes through, but he was so deep in his fury he never notices. If it was physically possible, he would have steam coming out of his ears. He was fuming. Stomping past me and opening his office door, he turns around and looks right at me.

"Leah!" I jump with fear as he shouts my name. His eyes soften when he sees my movements, speaking in a calmer tone this time. "In my office...." Already looking at the floor, I nod my head as I stand up, walking towards him. Damian steps to the side of the door, giving me room to come through. He has an energy about him that I can't place but I know whatever it is, it's not aimed at me.

I finally look up at Damian's face and all I see is concern. "Leah." He stops his sentence and thinks as he walks closer to the lounge where I have sat down and sits on the coffee table in front of me. He places his elbows on his knees and rubs his hands together, like he is figuring out how to word what he wants to say. "Leah... you can tell me it is none of my business but I am going to ask you anyway. What's going on with Mike?" Even the mention of his name makes my skin crawl and I am sure Damian can tell I'm not happy hearing it. I feel like I need to tell someone, but I don't think Damian is that person, and yet he makes me feel so safe... why? Why does this man who is essentially a stranger make me feel safer than I have ever felt? I feel fingers slide under my chin, gently tilting my head back so I am looking into Damian's eyes. "I..." I stumble over my words. I want to tell him the truth, but I just can't get the words out of my mouth. Instead, I sit in silence as tears threaten to spill down my cheeks. With pity written all over his face, "Leah. You can talk to me. I *want* to help you, but I can't if you don't let me." I sit on the couch not able to hold back the tears. Before anything can escape my mouth my phone starts ringing, taking my attention away from the eyes of the man in front of me. Reaching down into my pocket, I pull out the cell to see who saved me from blurting out my secret, only to see Michael's name flashing. Standing up and moving away from Damian as I answer the call. "Hey Michael. What's going on?" I can hear him breathing through the speaker and I know instantly he isn't happy. Looking over at Damian, I notice him looking back at me with concern in his eyes. Distracting myself, I speak again before Michael gets the chance, "Mike, are you ok? Did something happen? What's wrong?" Hearing a growl on the other end scares me into dropping my phone. Damian scurries to grab it and puts it on speaker, not giving me any choice but to allow him to listen to the conversation.

"Leah.." Mike starts as he takes a deep breath and releases it. "What the fuck did you do?" I'm confused. What is he talking about? I haven't done anything since he dropped me off. I mean he left me 20 minutes ago. I can't get into too much trouble in that amount of time. Mike's tone is making me nervous and I stammer as I try to get the words out. "I haven't done anything, you have just dropped me at work, Mike." He growled possessively through the earpiece.

"I am going to ask you a question, and you better fucking answer me truthfully." He speaks to me like I am a child, knowing that it takes me back to my childhood. "Did you go to your bosses house and fuck him?"

My eyes cut to Damian's, who is already looking at me with a hint of pity mixed in with something else, something I can't figure out.

"N..N..No , Mike. I mean I took him to his home because he was drunk and needed to shower and sleep it off, so yeah, I mean, I did that part. But I haven't had sex with him. Why would you even ask me that?" While his question has me fired up, he knows I won't be able to do anything about it, I am too broken. I was cracked before I got to Mike, but that 'man' had completely broken me, now no one will want me. "Your fucking boss, 'Mister fucking perfect' told me." I'm back to looking at Damian. That's what it is, it's guilt. He feels guilty. Did he really tell Mike we had slept together? He wouldn't know the hell Mike puts me through, if he did he wouldn't say anything that would piss Mike off. " Are you really going to tell me he was lying, Leah? Why would he lie about that? More to the point, why would he lie about doing it with *you*? I'm sure that man wouldn't even have to beg to get pussy, he wouldn't even look sideways at someone like you." Hatred seeped out of his mouth and over the phone, entering my brain in the hurtful and painful way it usually does, and once again making me feel that he is right. No other man will ever want me and I will never be needed the way a woman feels like she should be.

Damian pulls me from my thoughts by his movements. He takes the phone off speaker and moves towards the door before turning around and yells out, "*Leah!* Get off the phone please. We have a meeting in 20 minutes and I need you to set up for it since Maria is away today. No personal calls, we just don't have time right now." Putting the phone up to my ear with my shaky hand, I go to repeat what Damian told me. Not having to say anything before I hear Mike's voice on the other end. "Go to lover boy, Leah. We will talk about this later. I will be picking you up every day and dropping you off. It seems that I need to remind you who owns you." He says before hanging up on me. I can't hold myself up any longer and collapse on the floor in a heap, sobbing to myself. Damian runs over to me, picks me up and places me gently down on the couch, before laying his jacket over my tiny body. I hear him as he leaves, talking to Maria as he closes the door behind him. I don't know what he is saying to her but he isn't gone for long. I feel him as he sits on the floor next to my head and starts to move my hair away from my wet cheeks. His sweet gesture made the tears fall harder. I should be mad at him for telling Mike those lies, but in my heart of hearts I know he wouldn't say them like Mike took them.

I open my eyes but the world that was in front of me was blurry through my tears. I could see Damian with kindness written all over his handsome face, he was obviously concerned

"I'm sorry, Leah. I didn't say those words, but I may have

let him take what he wanted from what I did say." He looks to the floor, shaking his head, ashamed of what has happened. There is no way he can know what trouble he has caused and I have no idea what will happen when Mike picks me up tonight.

I know he won't be happy. I will tell him I will meet him outside so he won't come in and cause a scene, I'm already embarrassed enough and Damian is the only one who has seen me. I can't have Mike coming in here and trying to start a fight with my boss; my boss who has been nothing but kind to me.

Leaning up on my forearm, slowly making my way to sitting upright, I can feel the tension that is coming from Damian. I know he is resisting the urge to ask me questions that I am just not ready to answer and it's like he knows I'm not.

"Leah." He sighs and I look towards him. I can't look him in the eyes, I am too embarrassed, but he grabs my chin, forcing me too.

"Leah, I don't know what is going on with you and Mike, but I am going to be honest, I don't like the way you look scared when he is around or even when he's only on the phone." He still hasn't let go of my chin and that is making it hard to hide the feelings that I know he can see on my face. One thing I have always been told is if my mouth doesn't tell you how I feel, then my face certainly will. Damian exhales, "Leah, I know something is going on, but I understand you don't want to talk about it. I want you to know that when you are ready to talk to someone, my door is open. I want you to talk to me about it. I can help, whatever it is. I have money if that is what you need and I know people that can help. Whatever it is, when you are ready, I will do everything I can to help."

This man, who in the grand scheme of things, barely knows me, wants to waste his money helping me. I am baffled, I am a nobody, I am not special, I am not someone he should save.

"Mr. Caldwell, I appreciate your concern and your offer, but there are people out there who deserve to have your help, I, however, am not one of them." Standing myself up and straightening my clothes, I walk over to the mirror fixing my makeup before opening the door and leaving his office, quietly closing the solid wood behind me.

CHAPTER 14

Damian's POV

"Leah." I sighed at her as she looked at me. She doesn't look me in the eyes. I know that she is embarrassed, I don't ever want her to feel that way around me so I do the one thing I can think of and I grab her chin, forcing her to look me in my eyes. I want her to know that she is supported.

"Leah, I don't know what is going on with you and Mike, but I am going to be honest, I don't like the way you look scared when he is around or even when he's only on the phone." I don't give her a chance to look away as I keep holding her chin. I can see that it is making it hard for her to hide the way she feels, I can see it on her face. Exhaling, I continue. "Leah, I know something is going on, but I understand you don't want to talk about it. I want you to know that when you are ready to talk to someone, my door is open. I want you to talk to me about it, I can help, whatever it is. I have money if that is what you need and I know people that can help. Whatever it is, when you are ready, I will do everything I can to help."

I can see the pain in her eyes, she is hurting and there is nothing I can do about it right now when all I want to do is make her smile.

"Mr. Caldwell, I appreciate your concern and your offer, but there are people out there who deserve to have your help, I, however, am not one of them." I watch her as she stands up and straightens her clothes down then walks over to the mirror fixing her makeup before opening the door and leaving my office, quietly closing the solid wood behind her.

I sit in the one spot, gobsmacked. What does she mean 'she doesn't deserve my help?' Why would she think that? She is one of the most kindest hearted people I have had the pleasure of meeting. I am man enough to acknowledge that I have developed some kind of feelings for her, what they are I am not too sure. I want to protect her, I want to help her, I want to save her. I have never had these feelings before, not even for Marisha, who I thought I was going to spend the rest of my life with.

I have made it clear to her she can come to me when she is ready for help, whatever kind of help it happens to be. The thought of her needing help in the first place makes me feel stabbing pains through my heart and I can't stop the few tears that seem to escape down one cheek.

Pulling my emotions back into check, I walk out the door pretending like I wasn't just sitting on the floor crying over a woman who doesn't want me but I just can't seem to let go of.

Clearing my throat, "Ah, Maria. Can I talk to you for a minute? Um, in my office please." Holding the door open for Maria as she walks through, I gently close it behind her and signal to the couch. I don't know what I am going to say but I need to talk to someone and Maria is like a mother to me, she can give me advice.

But before I get to even sit down she speaks up. "Damian. I know you want to help her, but she isn't ready for it. Give her time... Please." The tone in Maria's voice makes me think she knows more than she is saying but I don't press her for any information. All I can do is sit and stare at this woman, my mind racing on what could actually be happening in Leah's life and how much worse I have just made it for her.

"I... I don't know much. I've picked up on stuff, seen some things. She has mentioned a couple of things but I swore I wouldn't say anything and I intend to keep that promise. I want to help her too, but we have to wait. Okay?"

I start shaking my head, "I think I fucked up, Maria. Well no, I know that I have fucked up really bad." Maria quickly turns her head to face me and I look her in the eyes. The eye contact was so powerful I nearly fell off the side of the couch. "I think I have put her in an even more dangerous situation and I don't think I can fix it." Maria reaches over, grabbing my hand and squeezing it tight.

"We will help her with whatever is going on. We just need to let her tell us in her own time. Listen, son. We will keep watch over her, start taking note of anything odd. Eventually, she will be ready and we will be waiting, okay?" She slides her palm down my cheek. The touch is gentle and sweet. "But for now, we better get back to work, we have a pitch in 2 hours and we need you to put your game face on."

Nodding at her, I know what she is saying is right, but I am struggling to just push Leah to the back of my mind. I can't. This woman is always on my mind lately and I have no idea how to stop it and now it is even worse, knowing something is going on with Mike is making me feel angry. Angry and useless.

Sitting at the huge table on the opposite side of the potential clients, I am still thinking about Leah. Thinking about what I heard and even worse, what I didn't. She isn't off her game though. The clients love her and it's easy to understand why. She has this way of making everyone feel important. From the CEO down to the person running the mail, everyone is exactly the same. She doesn't deserve whatever is happening behind the scenes. I'm brought from my thoughts by everyone at the table standing up and shaking hands. I get a pang of jealousy as I watch Leah as she talks to the CEO and our high profile potential client, John Kowalski. She gives him a sweet smile and starts waving him off as he walks over to me, extending his hand towards mine.

"Pleasure as always, Damian." I take his hand in mine and we shake. I watch him as he turns, looking back at Leah, passion flooding his eyes before he looks back at me and I know instantly what he is thinking about and I can't stop the scowl I give him. Throwing his hands up in surrender. "Sorry man, didn't know she was taken already. Stepping back."

"No, it's ok. She isn't mine, she is just my PA." I reply, nodding as I try to convince myself of what I'm saying. John laughs, "Alright man, Maybe your brain should tell the rest of your body then." It is then that I realise I have curled my palms into fists and standing tall, ready for a fight and everyone is looking at me. God... This can't get any worse.

CHAPTER 15

Leah's POV

I feel like we have been at this for hours. Once again I stand up from the table that we have been using. It is full of papers that are spread out covering the whole surface. Settling in for the long haul, I slip my feet out of my black wedge shoes and give my toes a little wiggle, stretching them out after being stuffed in those heels all day. Maria looks over at me, "Feet hurting, darling?" I give her a small smile as I nod and rub the soles of my feet at the same time.

"How about we take a break? I have a feeling this is going to be one of those late nights I warned you about when I hired you." I watched Damian as he spoke and looked up at me through his lashes, his hazel eyes shining through them. They are so clear I can see the emerald and gold flecks that flitter through. I feel like I could stare at them all day long.

My attention is taken away from his eyes by a commotion that seems to be coming from out at reception. Damian starts to walk out of the room and towards the shouting as I follow him out the doors and closer to the noise. As we walked up to the scene, Damian pushed me even further behind him. His big body protecting mine from any potential threat. The move seemed seamless and natural, and it gave me butterflies thinking why he would do that. I grab onto the back of his shirt, scrunching my palms into fists so I won't get lost if there is any kind of brawl. Damian came to a complete stop in front of me and I was walking so close behind him that I ran into his solid back. I am so close to him I can feel his body shaking. What is happening? Panic started to run through my veins and I was close to breaking down. Damian turns his head, looking down at me with a smile on his face until he sees the panic running through my body.

Quickly he steps aside allowing me to see that the commotion isn't what I expected it to be. Instead it is one of my fellow workers standing in the middle of the office in a puddle of water and ice cubes laughing so hard he is bent over and crying.

Not being able to help myself, I burst out laughing too. I was laughing so hard I fell into Damian's chest. He grabbed me as I fell into him and I could feel how fast his heart was beating as I stared into those beautiful Emerald orbs. Damian lifted his hand and moved the hair from my face, tucking it behind my ear and all of a sudden it was like we were all alone in the office. Just him and I. I desperately want to kiss him and I have a feeling he feels the same way. The tension floating around us right now is electric and everyone around us has noticed. Someone coughed and broke me away from Damian. I looked over at my coworkers whose mouths were wide open and staring at us. I cleared my throat and went to step back. As I do, I hear a familiar voice call my name.

"Leah!" My eyes widen and my heart started pounding. I turned quickly and faced the person who called out and it was exactly who I thought it was, *Micheal.*

I was terrified of what his reaction would be. I stumbled backwards as Michael stormed towards me. Damian caught me before I fell too far and put me behind him again.

"Micheal!" Damian says with such power, Micheal stopped in his tracks. Damian's tone now is calm. "Micheal. Can we help you?" Micheal looked at me, "Yeah, I told Leah I would pick her up tonight." His jaw clenched as he spoke. I step out from behind Damian and head towards Mike. A gentle voice from behind me speaks, "She has only just found out we are all working late tonight. She probably hasn't had a chance to let you know." I turn and look at the person who is speaking and I can tell Maria is trying to dig me out of the shit. I turn to Michael again and start to walk forward, I can tell he is starting to really get agitated, I can see it in his eyes. He tries to reach out and grab my arm, but I take his hand in mine to try and defuse the situation.

"I am so sorry, Mike. I would have told you but I found out not long ago myself and didn't have the chance to let you know yet." The anger is swelling on the surface and it only gets worse when I feel a body standing close behind me. I don't need to turn around to see who it is, Mike's reaction tells me all I need to know.

"Sorry mate, I just sprung this on all of them not long ago. None of them have had a chance to let their families know. But don't worry, I make sure all my staff get home safe when they work long hours." Damian steps around me, stands beside me and puts out his hand. "It was good to see you again Mike." As he takes Mike's hand and shakes it, he turns to the crowd that had gathered around us and speaks up. "Alright everyone, fun is over, let's get back to work. We need to get this ready for tomorrow." Waving his hands out in front of him, motioning for everyone to leave. Damian however, doesn't leave. Instead, he turned back around and looked at Mike. "Sorry mate, we have work to do. Leah will see you later. Come on Leah." He says pointing to the office. "Maria! Come on!" he yells out afterwards. Mike shook his head and clenched his jaw even more - if that was even possible. I watched him walk away towards the elevator, stopping in front, waiting for the doors to slide open.

Once I see him walk in and disappear, Damian and Maria grab me and walk me into his office and sit me down on the couch, holding onto me as I sit. Damian started pacing the floor, with his hands on his hips and looking down. He stopped suddenly, squats down in front of me and says gently.

"Leah, I know I said I wouldn't push you, but I just need to know. Are you in danger?" He is looking at me with hope in his eyes. I'd like to think I wasn't ready to tell him what has been happening to me at home. I had never felt comfortable enough with anyone to say the words out loud but I find the words start to fall from my lips.

"I... I.... It is not nice, Damian." Tears well in my eyes and I can't stop them from falling as I stumble through my words. Breaking down, Damian takes my hands in his.

"Does he hurt you, Leah? In any way whatsoever?" My head drops and my shoulders start to shake. All I can do is nod my head and doing that is like opening the floodgates. I can't stop myself from falling into Damian as I cry. He fell to the ground as he wrapped me up in his arms and allowed me to have my feelings without any more talking.

Damian's POV

I watched the tears roll down Leah's cheeks before she fell into my chest, knocking us both to the ground. My arms instinctively wrapped around her and held her tight to me. I looked up at Maria who also had tears running down her face and the gravity of what Leah was telling me without saying anything hit me. Instantly, I was angry. I wanted to beat this so-called man, but for right now, I am going to sit here and let Leah cry. I gently rub my fingers in a soothing motion up and down her spine trying to get her to calm down and after a few minutes, it seems to work. She starts to regulate her breathing as she sits up, slowly I move my fingers under her chin and lift them so I can see her face.

"Leah, you don't have to worry anymore, I will protect you. We need to get you out of that house and somewhere safe and we will have to be clever about it. I know men like Mike and he won't let you go easily. This could take a while." I look at her directly, switching between her eyes. "Do you think you can hold on while we sort this out? I will do anything to get you out safely." I take a deep breath and look at Maria who is nodding at me with a small smile on her face. I desperately want to kiss Leah, right here, right now. But this is not the time or place so I just pull her into my chest again. I just need her close, I need to feel like I am able to do something for her and at this very moment, this is what I can do for her.

CHAPTER 16

Michael's POV

Sliding into the driver's seat, I slam the door shut and proceed to punch the steering wheel of the car. Accidentally hitting the horn several times I drew unwanted attention from the passers-by and all I can do is smile and give them a small wave, letting them know all is ok. Really though, I would rather flip them the bird and tell them all to fuck off, but I can't have any attention on me. My plans for Leah may be going sideways right now, but I will roll with the punches and get the end I deserve somehow... I just need to think, I need to be smart. I can't have people remembering 'the weird aggressive guy in the parking lot'.

I took a deep breath, letting it out slow, trying my hardest to calm myself down.

As I turned the key and felt the car start up with a loud rumble, I start to reverse out of the parking spot only to catch Damian's other receptionist, Melanie or whatever her name is, crossing from out the front of the office building to the cafe across the road. I wonder what she is doing. Letting curiosity get the better of me, I pulled back into the park and watched her. For an older woman, she isn't too bad to look at and if I didn't have my girl already I would take her instead.

I can only just recognise her through the windows at the

front of the cafe as she stood at the counter talking to the worker on the other side.

She looks nervous, and I watched her as she looked over her shoulder again and again, like she can feel my eyes on her, drinking her in.

Unfortunately with her knowing Leah, I would never be able to convince her to fall for me. Leah was so easy to brainwash into thinking we were in love. She had spent her childhood unloved and unwanted. Bouncing from foster home to foster home, each one worse than the one before.

As soon as I saw her I knew she was the one, I could see how broken she was, how easy it would be to build her back up to believe what I told her. She was such a good girl for so long, that is until she got this job working for this cunt. He is ruining everything. I should just take him out, get it over with.

I started to think of ways to kill him without making myself a suspect but all his employees saw us arguing just now. I would be the first one the cops would want to talk to.

I don't like the way Damian looks at my Leah. He wants her, I can see it. But what is even worse is the way she looks at him. She has never looked at me like that, not willingly anyway.

I giggled to myself, thinking about all the times I forced her to her knees. Making her beg for me to take her as she sobbed and the tears rolled down her face. I remember the first time like it was yesterday. She had been in my possession for six months. I desperately wanted to play, but she didn't want to. Hearing her being defiant pissed me off, but also turned me on a little. I couldn't stop myself, hell, I didn't *want* to stop myself. The thought of taking her without consent thrilled me and I instantly got rock hard. Even now, having the memory makes my dick twitch in my pants. Maria walked out of the cafe and looked around, holding the cup tray with the 3 coffee cups held in it. She can feel my eyes on her, she knows someone is watching her. She doesn't know who and she doesn't know why, but she can feel it. I bet the hair on her neck was standing. The nervous energy flowing off her as she walked across the road, stopping in front of the office building before turning to look behind her one last time, making sure no-one was following her as she turned back towards the building and walked inside.

I finally turned the car back on and started to reverse out of the parking spot, stopping before the back of my car hit the front of another car. *Concentrate Michael.* I pushed the gear stick into first gear and revved the engine, spinning the wheels as I took off.

I needed to release some stress and there was only one person who was brave enough to let me do what I needed to.

I drove fast. Taking the road like it was a race track. Drifting from side to side as I take each corner until I finally pull up in front of my destination.

As I turned the key, turning the car off, I sat and looked up at the basic brick house. The bricks had been painted white, but not well. You could still see the dark from the brick itself under the paint. I wondered if her neighbours had any idea of what goes on inside those walls. I opened the door and got out, closing it behind me as I walked up the front path and onto the porch stopping in front of the door.

"Well, well, well. Look what the cat dragged in..." The familiar seductive voice came through the speaker next to the door frame and a grin appeared on my face. I lent on the frame and looked into the camera. "Are you going to let me in, baby?" My voice now is a drawl of need and want. "Or does a man have to knock this fucking door down before he can tie you up and take you?" The ideas I have for the play time I am about to have are my last straw and I shoulder barge the door open, barrelling into the foyer and coming to a complete stop a few feet from the entrance. Standing in front of me was the woman I was here to see and she had a nervous look on her face. And let me tell you, it was for good reason, what I have planned for her is nothing like I have ever done before.

CHAPTER 17

Leah's POV

I watched as Damian walked out the door with Maria, leaving me alone in the room. I turned to face the glass wall that looked out over the city and wondered if Mike was still close by.

The instant anger in Damian's eyes when I told him about Mike was crazy but reassuring. It made me feel safe, and that was not something I was used to feeling. I don't think Ive ever felt safe anywhere I had ever been.

I barely scratched the surface of what is happening between Mike and I with Damian and he is already this mad, I can't tell him any more. He would absolutely lose his mind if he knew the truth.

I watched the people on the ground from high above, wondering what kind of lives they lead. Are they happy? Sad? Trapped? Is there someone like myself down there? Someone who is doing whatever they have to to survive.

My attention is dragged away from my thoughts to the door of the office, the jiggling sound of the handle echoed around the room and I started to panic. I instantly thought it was Mike trying to get to me. The handle kept turning from side to side, like whoever it was couldn't get the door to unlock and open.

I ran and hid under Damian's desk, hoping not to be seen by the intruder.

I held my hands over my mouth, hoping that my heavy breathing didn't give away my hiding spot. I hear the door open and footsteps head in my direction. The sound was getting closer and closer when the person spoke up.

"Leah? Are you in here? Where are you?" The voice belonged to Damian and it was full of panic. I let my hands fall from over my mouth to the floor and started to sob uncontrollably. The tears rolling down my cheeks like a river flowing after a storm.

Damian comes running towards the sounds of my cries and drops to the floor and crawled under the desk, taking me in his arms before he is even fully settled in beside me.

"Leah? What's wrong? What happened?" The fear in his voice let me know once again that he cared. I tried to let him know that I thought it was Mike coming to get me when I heard him opening the door, but the words couldn't make it past the uncontrollable sobbing that was happening at that moment.

My entire body shook with adrenaline and I couldn't stop it. I felt like my time had stopped right when my fear peaked and I couldn't get it to go again, like I was stuck in this fate forever.

"Shhhhh, Leah. It is okay..." I felt Damian rub my back slowly, the movements were calming. "You are okay. I've got you and I won't let anything happen to you, I promise." I felt the emotion behind those last two words and they instantly made me feel safe. The shaking my body was experiencing started to slow and my mind started to calm. The rivers that had been flooding my cheeks flowed a little less and my breathing became more stable.

I pulled my head off of Damian's chest a little so I could see the man who has today alone, spent countless hours comforting me. I looked him in the eyes and all I saw was pity. He pitied me. Just what I didn't want. I didn't *need* him to pity me, I needed him to be my friend. Without thinking I crawled out from under the desk and stood up. I felt so angry. Angry at Damian for his pity. Angry at Mike for everything and angry at the world for allowing all these horrible things to happen to me.

I turned towards the office door and ran. I ran through the office cubicle and I couldn't tell if the tears that fell from my eyes were a side effect of how angry I was or if it was leftover from the adrenaline. Whatever they were from, they fell as I ran out of the building. I ran for what seemed like hours and when I had finally stopped running I looked around not recognising where I was and the panic I had run off was once again creeping in. I was turning in circles, my eyes jutting from building to building, trying my hardest to find anything familiar so I could keep hope that I haven't gotten myself lost.

I chose a direction to head in and I started walking. One foot in front of the other. As I walked it started to feel like someone was watching me but I never noticed anything suspicious as I looked at my surroundings. Old brick buildings lined each side of the street. They were decent sized and clean. Each front yard looked exactly the same, right down to the length the grass had been cut.

I wasn't concentrating on where I was walking when I ran into a big body. I grabbed onto the strong arms to steady myself and looked up at the person I had run into. "Shit, I'm so sorry." It was then I took notice of who was standing in front of me. My heart started pounding as the shock registered. This can't be happening. He can not be here. How did he know where I would be?

"Hey baby. Where are you off to in such a hurry?" A big

hand wrapped around my bicep, grabbing it hard and squeezing. "Hmmmm? Where were you running too?" The man started to pull me forward by my arm so violently I was sure I had instant bruising. We walked fast further up the street to a car that was parked on the kerbside. I was in a panic but I knew I couldn't let him see how he made me feel.

"How did you find me?" I said the words with absolute attitude in the hopes he wouldn't be able to see through them. He smirked and I couldn't stop the shiver that ran down my spine. He stepped closer making it so we were now chest to chest. Slowly, he lifted his hand and grabbed some of my hair, running it between his fingers before moving it behind my shoulder. He placed his fingers under my chin and lifted, forcing me to look at him. "Oh Leah. I know where you are always, don't think you are ever out of my sight." He moved his fingers from gently holding my chin to wrapping his hand under my chin to hold it in place as he bent down. I felt his lips touch mine and instantly I wanted to move away, but how he was holding my face made it so he had complete control over it.

He pulled away, his tone now an angry growl. "Now, get in the *fucking* car! And *do not* make a scene." I noticed his eyes were dark and full of anger as he pushed me into the passenger seat of the car. I wanted to scream. I wanted to let the strangers on the street know I wasn't safe and I needed help. But instead I did what was demanded, losing all hope... Losing the will to fight. This is my life, I don't know why I thought I could get away from it, but here it is in all it's glory. I looked out the car window as he pulled onto the road, looking at the people on the sidewalk, to them we just look like your normal couple out for a drive but I knew better. The horrors that were to come were nothing compared to what I had ever been through.

CHAPTER 18

Damian's POV

I just stood and watched. I watched as Leah burst into tears and ran out of here like she was scared. Like she was scared of *me*. I didn't understand what I said or did.

I started running through what happened, over and over again. Analysing every little detail. I walked in the door and I couldn't see Leah. I started calling out for her and that is when I heard the sobbing. I followed the sound to find Leah hiding under my desk with the seat pulled up tight to her body, hiding ninety percent of it. I climbed under there and sat with her, I let her tears soak my shirt. She looked up at me then whatever happened, happened.

I was pacing the floor in the middle of the room, the worry clearly showing. *Should I go after her? Where would she go? What did I do?*

I needed answers and I needed them now. I needed to find her to make sure she was ok.

I strode towards the door, yanking it open and running into Maria and almost bowling the poor woman over. My reflexes were fast and I managed to grab her by the top of her arms holding her steady. "*Fuck!* Sorry Maria." I let her go and started walking off on her. "Cancel everything for the rest of today, I have to go out." I can hear the light footsteps speeding up behind me as I stalked my way to the elevator door and slammed my hand on the button several times, the actions showing everyone in the office just how much I needed to get out of here. I needed to get outside, into the fresh air.

The doors to the elevator ding and opened up allowing me to slide through them before they had even finished opening and Maria managing to squeeze her skinny self through as well. She stood in front of me, her arms folded over her chest looking at me like I imagine a disappointed mother would look at her son.

"Damian." The tone of her voice told me how serious she was. "I know you want to find Leah." She paused and let her arms fall to her sides as she took a deep breath. "I know you want to make sure she is okay, but maybe... maybe you need to give her some space... just for a day or two, yeah?" The elevator stopped in the basement and I dropped my head as I walked out, "You don't understand, Maria. I *have* to find her. She was terrified... of me." I whispered the last part, the anger mixed with the sadness evident.

"Hey!" She yelled out as she chased after me. "Listen here. I know you like her, Damian, and I get it, I really do. But you can't just run out there looking for a woman that ran out of your office." Maria jumped in front of me, stopping me in my tracks. "Damian, I don't think you understand the gravity of what is happening right now." I can see her starting to get frustrated with me, something I have been doing more and more lately. "I don't understand what you mean, Maria." I was clearly confused. "She has feelings for you, Damian. It's obvious to everyone, including Mike, and that puts her in a difficult position. I have seen the change in her so surely Mike has too."

What Maria was trying to tell me finally clicked and the panic spread across my face. Maria reacted instantly, saying to me before I could do or say anything "I will call her, okay? I will call her and make sure she is okay." Her voice was back to being soft and kind just like the Maria I knew.

"Okay. But you have to do it now and put her on speaker. I want to hear her for myself."

I watched as she gently nodded her head and took her phone out of her pocket Unlocking it and scrolling through her contacts until she found Leah's number.

Tapping on Leah's name on the screen then the speaker, she held it out so I could see. It rung a few times before the sound of Leah's sweet voice filled the air around us.

"Hello, Maria? Is everything okay?" The concern in her voice was evident. I opened my mouth to talk and Maria threw her hand over my mouth. I looked down at her and saw her lips moving. I couldn't understand why she was mouthing 'Mike' when we were clearly talking to Leah. It was then that I heard the noise in the background. It sounded like someone was shuffling around close to the phone, like they were trying to listen into the conversation. I knew instantly it was Mike, I mean who else in her life would be this much of a psycho? He had found her. He got her. He got her because of me.

I dropped my head in devastation. Maria Spoke, breaking me from my thoughts. "Yes dear. Everything is okay. I just wanted to check in on you. Are you okay?" There was a short delay in Leah's answer, like she had to think about what she wanted to say instead of just answering the question. "I am fine Maria." She paused long enough for Maria to ask one more question. "Leah? Why did you leave work?" The question left Leah silent for a minute. "I wasn't feeling well so I went to Mr Caldwells bathroom for some privacy. When I was finished I came out and felt no better so I decided to get some fresh air. That's all. I just have been walking around the city trying to settle my stomach." Her voice was shaky and uneven and you could hear she was nervous about something... or someone.

Suddenly there was a loud noise coming through the phone's speaker and a scream, some yelling and then some crying before Leah's voice was back. "Sorry about that, I accidentally dropped my phone." I had my hands balled up into fists so much that my knuckles had turned white. I couldn't take it anymore and stormed off hearing Maria speaking to Leah as I walked away. I needed to get out of here, I needed to clear my head and there's only one place where I can do that....

CHAPTER 19

Leah's POV

As I sat looking down at my phone I couldn't help but wonder what is going to happen now. I did as he asked. I lied to my friends, I told them I was okay.

Truth is, I am so far from okay that even with a map I don't think I'd find it.

"Stop that bullshit right now, Leah!" I hear from In Front of me as he slaps the phone out of my hand. I turned my head away from him, refusing to let him see the tears but all that did was allow him to grab my chin tightly and violently turn my head back towards him. "You will *never* turn your head from me again. You hear?" I didn't want to answer him. I wanted him to die, instead I just made him more aggravated by my lack of response and removed his hand from my chin, slapping me across my face. Grabbing my chin again he bent down, looking me in the eyes, his face only millimetres from my own. "You hear me, you little cunt?" The venom dripped through his words as he spoke.

I looked back at him fiercely, not wanting him to know just how much he scared me. "I fucking got it, Mike." The attitude came flooding out of my mouth and anger flooded his eyes.

Mike let his grip fall from my chin to my neck and wrapped his hand around it, squeezing it tightly.

I struggled to get a full breath as he squeezed tighter. He bent closer to my face, giving me a smug grin as he then moved his mouth beside my right ear. "I. Fucking. *Own.*You, Leah." His words sent a shiver down my spine and I couldn't stop the movement before Mike noticed it, that was when he knew he had me.

He loosened his grip on my neck a little allowing me to take a deep breath. It was only a minute before he tightened it back up, pulled me up and threw me on my knees in front of him. I watched him as he let go of me and slowly moved his hands to his belt, undoing it and pulling it through the loops on his jeans. I watched as his hands moved, fear running through my veins. I knew what was about to happen, the pain that I was going to go through. I was defeated. I couldn't fight it anymore, I was mentally drained and nothing to fight for anyway.

Mike wrapped the belt around my neck, pulling on the end gently, restricting my airflow just enough to have an impact on how much oxygen my lungs could get.

He looked down at me with a look of pure pleasure on his face. Seeing me panic made him hard. Bending down and grabbing one of my hands which I had called into a fist, he opened it up and placed it on the front of his pants. I held my hand in the one spot as he let go of it and started to undo the button and zipper that held the denim up and let them slide down his legs. Grabbing my hand which had fallen when his pants had, he brought it back up and sat it on top of the material that was between his hard cock and my palm.

"Mmmmmm. Do you feel what you do to me, Leah? Feel how hard you make me when you disobey?"

With my hand motionless in its place, he started to move his hips, back and forth using my hand to jerk him off even though I literally wasn't doing anything.

"Mmmm, Leah. Your hand feels so good wrapped around my dick, baby. I bet your tight cunt will feel even better though."

My eyes widened with shock. I didn't want to have sex with him again, he disgusted me, but the smug look on his face says he wants it.

He tried to lay me down but, for the first time in a long time, I resisted and it took him by surprise.

Slapping him across his face, I screamed out. "Mike, stop it! No!" My cries were met with more aggression. The more I struggled and said no the more he enjoyed it. After a good five-minute struggle, he flipped me onto my stomach and pinned me down. Finally, he managed to get my panties off, dragging them down my legs and running his fingers over my skin as he did. I tried to wiggle my way out from under him but he was so much stronger than I was and I failed. I went limp as he plunged 3 of his fingers into my pussy. My body and mind went numb, I tried to block out what was happening but I failed. I could still feel his fingers inside me, I could hear him breathing behind me and I could tell he had that fucking look on his face. The one that he gets when he is forcing me to do what he wants even thought he knows I do not want to.

Mike grabbed my hair in his fist and yanked my head back as he slammed himself into my ass. I screamed out in pain and he roughly pulled out. "Leah." He thrusted his dick into my pussy. "Leah, you know I don't like to have to use lube. You know I like to be covered in your natural juices, baby." Angrily he kept going in and out, grunting each time he did.

Tears started to fall from my eyes and I hoped he hadn't noticed, I wasn't that lucky. He rubbed his thumbs down my cheeks, drying them, still fucking me from behind. "Little slut, the moisture is coming from the wrong part of your body. Although I do like it when you cry, It gets me so fucking hard." Taking his cock out of my pussy he slammed himself back into my ass. The pain was too much and I screamed out again. Why me? Why do these things happen to me?

I felt him finish inside me and I knew he was done and would be asleep in seconds. Waiting to hear him snoring I got out of the bed and headed for the shower. There is not enough soap to wash this man off my skin but I have to try. I snuck past the kitchen, grabbing the steel wool from the sink and I ran to the bathroom, closing the door behind me quietly and leaning on the back of it.

I have to find a way out of this Hell. I have tasted freedom and I want more.

Chapter 20

Damian's POV

I sat in my office staring out of the windows that divided me from the rest of the workers, wondering where Leah was. It had been an entire week since she ran out of here frightened and crying. I couldn't help the feeling that kept rising from the Pit of my stomach each time I thought of her. I couldn't figure out where she had gone.

I had ignored Maria's advice and I had driven around looking in all the places that I had heard her mention in conversations before but I had had no luck.

The door flew open, the sudden movement giving me a scare and my body jumped a little out of the chair.

"What the fuck, Damian!" The high pitched squawk instantly alerted me to who had just stormed into my office unannounced. I rolled my eyes ready for the abuse that was about to be hurled my way. "Damian Caldwell! Don't you *dare* roll your eyes at me!" As I looked toward the screeching I noticed the cunt wasn't alone. Why the *fuck* she needed to bring the rest of the coven of cunts, I have no idea. Standing up from behind my desk, I walked around the edges and clenched my fists, trying to stop myself from beating the life out of this so called woman and her rodent friends. I bit down hard and spoke through my teeth. "Oh hey Marisha, how are you?" She opened her mouth to respond but I held my hand up letting her know I didn't actually want an answer. "Believe it or not, I don't want to hear what you have to say." I stepped closer to her so we were almost touching chests and she gave me a smile. The kind of smile that would scare the devil. The kind of smile that told me she was up to something.

Raising an eyebrow I questioned her, "what is going through that head of yours, Marisha? Hmm??" The tone of my voice was monotone with a hint of aggression but the smile sat firmly planted on her face as she moved forward ensuring our bodies were touching and lifted a hand, placing it on my pec.

Her fingers expanded over my chest as she lifted her other hand and grabbed my chin roughly and tilted my head down, forcing me to look at her. She knew me well.... Too well. Marisha let go of my chin and allowed her hands to run down my chest, her touch making me feel physically sick. "You wanna know what is going through my head?" She purred as she let her hands glide further south, coming to a stop close to my belt buckle. I moved quickly and grabbed her hands, stopping them from going any further south. "Marisha." I mumbled through gritted teeth. "How many times do I have to say to you that I hate you?" I threw her hands to the side of us and let them go mid air.

She started to laugh, the sound piercing my ears causing me to grimace.

"You say you hate me, Damian, but how many times have you come back to me? Begging me to allow your cock inside me?" She palmed my dick through my pants and I cursed myself as a moan left my lips. "You may hate me, but I am the only woman who can take what you offer, who will let you *fuck* the way you like to... the only one who will put up with your shit." As she looked down at her hand, still rubbing my now semi hard cock and smiled she continued, "see baby? Your dick knows it wants me, so why can't you just admit it?" She licked up the side of my neck and it broke me out of whatever trance she had once again put me under.

I stepped back from her, denying her body the skin she so desperately wanted to have pressed against her and shook my head. "My dick is a whore, Marisha. It would fuck anything." The hurt shone from her eyes briefly before she gathered herself and stepped away, heading back towards her friends. Stopping when she got to them, she turned to face me and I knew what she was feeling instantly, it was written all over her face. I had never seen her so angry and the look in her eyes as she stared my way, terrified me. I knew this woman, I knew her and I knew how vindictive she could be and the unpredictability of her scared me. Marisha spoke up, her voice darker than I had ever heard it. "You have no idea what I am capable of, Damian Caldwell. I always get what I want...." She paused and that was when I noticed how quiet it truly was in my office. "One way or another, D. I will get what I want." She gave me one last look-over from head to toe before she turned and took her attitude riddled ass out of my office and hopefully out of my building.

I exhaled, not realising until this moment that I had been holding my breath. Something inside me told me to forget her and what she said, I mean the woman is nuts... the other part told me to imagine how bad she could ruin my life AND my company... The thought terrified me. I needed to let off some steam and there was only one way I could do that and be satisfied.

Slapping the intercom on the phone that sat on top of my desk and waited for it to connect, I thought about Leah. Why can't I get this girl off my mind? Maria's voice broke my train of thought. "Yes Sir?" I noticed the concern in her voice.

"Make the call, Maria. I will be leaving in 5, have the car ready and waiting for me downstairs please."

Before she had the chance to confirm my request back to me, I hung up the phone and took long strides towards the door that led me out of my office. I swung the door open, I needed to get out of here....*NOW!*

Chapter 21

Damian's POV

As I sat in the backseat of the town car I looked up at the brick building. I contemplated asking the driver to take me home, but I was itching to smell the mixture of blood, sweat and leather.

I leant forward and touched the driver on the shoulder, "I'll call you when I'm ready." He looked back at me through the revision mirror and simply nodded. "Good man." I said as I gently slapped his shoulder a couple of times.

I opened the car door and slid my way out of the backseat. Standing tall and shutting the door, I watched the car drive off as I buttoned up my suit jacket, the collar of my blood red shirt showing.

I casually walked up to the door, grabbing the silver door handle once again. *It's been a while old friend.* I thought as I turned the knob and walked through the framework. The door let out a small moan, an indication of what sounds happens inside and I smirked a little. *Those sounds won't be happening in my room, not without my say so.*

"Good afternoon, we have your guest set up in your usual room." I nodded at the gentleman and as we walked through the halls to the same room I always got I listened to him talk. I wasn't sure what he was talking about but I seemed to have nodded and smiled in all the right places. My mind was focused on what it wanted to do, no.... What it needed to do to Victoria.

Stopping in front of room five I said thank you to the gentleman and watched him walk back down the hall eventually turning a corner and out of sight.

I grabbed the handle and swung the door open to see Victoria on the floor on her knees. Her head was down and facing the floor. She was ready and waiting for me. I undid the button on my jacket and slid it down my arms, catching it before it fell onto the floor and throwing it over the chair that sat to the right of me as I walked towards her, stopping so close to her that the tips of my shoes were only millimetres from touching her knees. "You are such a good girl, aren't you, sweets?" I knelt down in front of her and placed my fingers softly under her chin and lifted so she would have to look at me. While she was distracted I placed my other hand on the inside of her thigh and started to push it upwards. I watched as Victoria registered what I was doing and her eyes grew wider. Biting her lower lip to stop herself from making any noises as my fingers inched closer to her clit, stopping at their destination with a slight touch on her sensitive spot.

She worked hard to remain silent, knowing that was one of my demands. I brought my face closer to hers as I slid the tips of my fingers over pussy, I could feel how wet she already was for me.

"Off your knees and go lay face down on the bed. Your ass looks pale, I believe it needs some..." I grinned at her and continued, "colour." I roughly pulled her face closer to mine by her chin, kissing her with force before I bit her bottom lip. It instantly started to bleed a little. I watched as the blood started to run down her chin from her lip slowly, a single drop travelling on an adventure.

I let gravity take the drop closer to the floor before I flattened out my tongue, licking up the mess I caused. It tasted delicious. It was a taste I had almost forgotten. Something about it tasted different though.

Pushing the thought aside, I pulled back looking Victoria in the eyes. "On the bed Sweets, I'm getting hungry." I chuffed at her.

I stood up, turning around and heading towards the mirror that took up one whole side of the wall. Victoria knew I was watching her so she put on a show for me. I watched as she slunk her way to the bed and slid over the top of it, poking her sexy ass in the air and slowly spread herself out awaiting her next instruction.

"You are such a good girl, Victoria. I believe you deserve a treat." I started towards the cupboard and opened the doors wide, taking my time to look over my tools. I pulled out a flogger and ran the leather through my fingers. Excitement started to run through my veins as I turned and walked over to the bed. Seeing Victoria spread out and vulnerable reminded me of the trust she had for me, that what we had here wasn't anything remotely romantic, but purely something to give us both the release we wanted, that we needed to get us through.

As I slowly lifted my arms grabbing hold of the suspenders that sat on top of my shoulders, I watched Victoria wiggle her ass at me, teasing me.

Sliding the suspenders down my arms, I calmly comment, "careful with the teasing, sweets. It won't work well for you today. I am in the mood to deal out punishments as it is."

I dropped them, letting them hang from the top of my black slacks as I rolled the sleeves of my shirt up my arms, showing off the artwork I had spent years getting done.

Once I was satisfied with the placement of the sleeves on my arms I made my way to the bed, stopping when I was standing in between Victoria's feet as they hung off the side.

Bending down slightly I ran my fingers over the bottoms of her feet, from her toes to the heels and over her Achilles, my gentle touch making her entire body shiver with pleasure. I knew she would be ready for me but tonight I was going to take my time and I knew Victoria wouldn't complain. She liked to hand over control as much as I liked to take it.

I spread my fingers out over her calf muscles and lightly pushed them further up the back of her legs, noticing her breath quicken and I knew I was getting her excited. "You are being such a good girl, Victoria. You may get something special if you keep this up, would you like that, hmm?" I saw her head nod but she still didn't make a sound like the obedient little sub she was.

I lifted my hand, bringing it down onto the soft flesh of her juicy ass. I watched it jiggle around my hand feeling the skin on mine made me hard and I knew I had to be inside of her.

Sliding backwards off the bed, I stood as I spoke my demand. "Off the bed and on your knees in front of me." I pointed to the spot in front of where I was standing, showing her exactly where I needed her. She slid off the bed and to the spot I pointed to, a giant grin on her face as she looked up at me through her lashes. She looked at the zipper on my pants then back up to me, asking me with her eyes if she could help herself to what was being restrained by the material that covered it. "Unzip my pants, take out my cock and let me shove it down your throat, sweets." It took her no time to do as I had asked. The zipper on my pants was undone, my underwear pulled down just far enough to be able to let my dick out and she shoved it into her mouth, making the most intense sounds as she sucked.

I watched her head move up and down on my cock, she made her lips touch the base and she gagged. I watched as the tears started to fall from her eyes leaving her mascara running down her face. The sight of her on her knees with my dick in her mouth and her face a mess made me harder than I had ever been for her and that is when I realised I was imagining Leah's face looking up at me. I grabbed her by the hair on the back of her head and yanked on it, pulling her head away from my body. "Are you ready for your treat, sweets?" Her eyes were wide as she awaited my instructions. "On your back on the bed, ass on the edge." I watched her as she hurried to do as she was told. Laying with her knees bent so just the heels of her feet were on the bed I could observe her pussy, dripping with anticipation of what was to come for her. I got on my knees in front of her, palming her thighs, "Wider." I demanded, her body instantly responded, her legs moving wider, allowing me to run my tongue from her asshole up to her clit, just one single time. I pulled my head away, licking my lips as I did. Her pussy dripped for me so much with one lick that it had made a mess of my face.

"Oh, sweets. You are already dripping for me, making quite the mess on the bed, aren't you?" I slid two of my fingers over her clit heading south, collecting her juices as I did making it easier to just slide my fingers into her opening.

I could feel her tighten around them, like her body did want to ever let go of the pleasure they gave. Slowly, I bent my fingers inside her as if I was telling her to 'come' here and instantly I felt her get wetter. I pulled my fingers out, not being able to take it anymore, and put them up to her lips. "Taste yourself." I demanded. Victoria wrapped her lips around what I offered her and sucked... hard. Reminding me of earlier when she had my cock in her mouth, making me moan. "Over... Now! And ass in the air, I am going to use your own juices to fuck you with a dildo in your ass while I fuck your cunt." Standing up, I walked over to the toy cupboard looking for the dildo I wanted. I turned to look at Victoria and saw she had already flipped herself over, her tight asshole calling to me, telling me to hurry up.

Grabbing hold of the first plastic dick I saw I strode over to her,slapping her other ass cheek and leaving a beautiful hand print on it. *That is going to show for days.* Placing the tip of the dildo at the entrance of her pussy I pushed it in. I heard her make a squeaky sound, obviously trying not to make any noise but failing. After pulling it out and pushing it back in a few times I pulled it out for the final time and sat it on her asshole, slowly pushing it inside her. I watched as the dildo slid through the hole, the images something one would never forget. Getting it all the way in, I started to run the tip of my dick over her sopping pussy. "I am going to fill these holes, Victoria." I slid my hard cock inside her as I said her name, moaning as I felt her wetness surround me.

As always, Victoria had her long hair tied back, making it easier for me to wrap it around the palm of my hand and pull her backwards, allowing me to get deeper into her pussy. I start to fuck her hard and fast, using her hair to pull her back onto me as I slam myself back into her, doubling the friction and making both of us groan. I stopped momentarily to grab her around the front of her neck and pull her up to me. I started to fuck her again, this time hard and slow making sure to pause after I pull out each time before slamming back into her. I moved my mouth closer to her ear, grunting to her, "Are you my good little whore? Hmmm, sweets? Do you like it when Daddy fucks you hard?" I was fucking her fast and knew I needed to slow down if I wanted to get everything out, making the most of the situation, it had been the longest time I had ever gone between sessions and my mind and body could feel it, they needed it.

I pulled out and laid underneath her, pulling her pussy down onto my mouth. Her juices leaking all over my face and the combination of my spit and her wetness making a mess all over the bed.

Pulling my head away from her, I mumbled, "Victoria, you are close, aren't you? I can feel it, you are literally dripping all over my face." Raising my arms between her legs, I put them up over her ass and pulled her back down onto my face, licking, sucking and slurping, making her squirm. Victoria started to move, grinding her clit as I sucked.

She was just about there, just about to cum. I pulled away again. "Oh now Victoria, you don't get to come just yet. You need to finish with me inside you and only when I say you can." I slid myself out from under her and knelt behind her flipping her onto her back before walking over to the cupboard that concealed the fun. *Now, what could accompany my flogger?* I grabbed the leather bound handcuffs and blindfold, walking back over to her and grinning as I got closer. "Oh sweets, you have no idea what beast you have with you tonight... Do you?" I said as I put the handcuffs on. "This is going to be a fun night for us both..."

Chapter 22

Damian's POV

I sat at the bar as I watched everyone around me play. The sounds of skin slapping on skin, the moans, the gagging and gurgling and the grunts. My eyes stop on a couple in a dark corner, the pair of them completely naked. Their bodies are in complete darkness leaving them looking like silhouettes. I watched as he bent her over the arm of an antique looking seat and used her hips as grab rails, thrusting his cock inside of her. I swirled the amber liquid that sat in the short glass as I watched them fuck. Every time the guy's cock was pushed inside her, her body would push further over the chair, forcing her to stretch her arms out in front of her, trying to get some kind of grip, and making her tits bounce... I watched her intently. The way her ass cheeks rippled each time her partners hand would strike them, the way her hands looked as they held onto whatever they could find just to stop her from being fucked onto the floor. It was those thoughts that made my dick hard.

I took a swing from my glass, not able to take my eyes off the couple. As erotic as it all was I had a feeling something was off. It bugged me enough that I stood up and headed toward the front door. I looked at the couple for one last time as I passed them, there was enough light now that I was closer to them to make out their features. The man looked up, shock registered on his face for a brief moment before he gave me a smug smile and brought the palm of his hand down onto the woman's ass once more. The slapping sound took over the room, drawing most people's attention to the corner. The scream that came from the lips of the woman wasn't one of pleasure but instead one of pure agony. The sounds seemed to spur the man on, the smug smile that stretched across his face as he pulled his cock out of the woman's pussy and slammed it into her asshole all the while looking at me. There was something about the man that seemed familiar, like someone I had met before. I looked down to the woman he was fucking and noticed the tears that ran down her cheeks. My eyes widened with the realisation of who the man was and what was happening. Instantly my hard on deflated and anger replaced the lust I had been feeling just minutes before.

TL WREN

I started to storm towards the couple, "Mike!" I yelled out, my anger seeping through my words, "Mike, you fucking cunt!" Mike looked back up at me, the smug smile still planted across his face and he continued to pound into Leah. Seeing her cry from the pain he was causing her made me ropable and almost unstoppable. Security stepped in front of me, trying to intimidate me even though I physically towered over them all.

I desperately wanted to barge them out of the way, run over to Leah, throw her over my shoulder like a caveman and run... I ran different scenarios on how I could get past the three buff mean looking men standing between me and her through my mind as I stared Mike down as he still fucked her. With his eyes still locked onto mine, he grabbed one of Leah's nipples, pinching it hard making her scream out in pain yet again, the scenario as a whole got the better of me and I lost it. The anger I had for this man exploded and I leapt towards him, grabbing him around the throat and restricting his airflow. I could feel the security team trying to grab me, trying to pull me away from this cunt, they weren't able to get my hands off him for about two minutes... not long enough for him to die.

Utter disappointment ran through my veins as it met the anger and the two emotions intertwined. My breathing was heavy as my chest rose and fell hard, showing the ever growing crowd that surrounded us just how much effort I had put into trying to take him out.

I felt a hand gently get placed on my heaving chest and I finally broke eye contact with Mike. Looking down, I looked into Leah's eyes and saw the hurt and fear that swirled in them. She opened her mouth to speak, "Please, Damian." She looked at the floor and sighed in defeat.

"Please don't. I am fine. You just need to leave me alone. I will be back at work next week, until then you won't hear from me." She stepped backwards and then again, falling onto the armchair she was just getting fucked over and turned her head away from me.

With frustration I threw my arms in the air, shaking security off me before I glanced one last time at Leah and shaking my head in disbelief. *I can't believe this, she wants to stay here... with this pathetic excuse of a man.*

I started to storm my way towards the front door, throwing it open with anger and almost ripping it off its hinges. Stomping my way down the front steps I looked around for the car only to remember I told him I would call him when I was ready. The thought had slipped my mind with everything else that had happened.

"Fuck!" I yelled out, the sound bouncing off the walls of the brick buildings that lined the oldest part of the city.

I started my way down the street, heading towards the city itself and away from the one place I wanted to be, the one person who I wanted to protect, the one person who *needed* me to protect them. Knowing I had just walked away and left her there with *him* made my anger start to boil over. *Fucking Mike.*

Pulling my phone out of my pocket I dialled for a car, sitting on the sidewalk as I waited I ran back through what Leah had said. *She was fine? She wanted me to leave her alone? Fucking fine, Leah.*

CHAPTER 23

Leah's POV

As the words fell from my mouth I watched Damian's face switch. The anger that had been flooding out of him slowly started to change as the pain of my words I had said sunk in. I had hurt him and in turn that hurt me. It pained me worse than anything Mike could ever do to me. My heart broke at that moment into a million little pieces that will never heal again.

I watched as he walked away, the one man who has ever done anything kind and not expected anything in return is leaving and it is all my fault. I could feel my heart start to race with each step he too and my chest started to heave. I placed my hand over my heart, convinced the pain I felt was a heart attack.

I sat up suddenly, blinking my eyes quickly. I soon figured out it was a dream.

I let out a breath as I lowered my head into my hands, *how many times am I going to have to relive that moment? How long am I going to torture myself?* I felt a hand grab me around my upper arm and once again I was reminded that I was not in a dream, that my life *IS* in fact very much a nightmare.

"Leah, lay down." Mike demanded, his voice was sleepy and gruff but forceful. I knew if I didn't do as he said he would make my life more unbearable then the hell I've been living.

As I laid down, I turned away from Mike, I didn't want to see him, I hated him. His hand touched my back, "oh, Leah. You think I care that you don't want to sleep facing me? Babe, I don't care that you don't like me, why would this bother me. You are here because I want *you*. What I want I take or take out anyone who gets in my way." His last words gave me chills. I knew he was talking about Damian. It had been a couple of months since I had seen him at the club. Since that night, Mike had made me resign from my job, threatening to kill Damian and Maria if I didn't.

I am his prisoner once again, and with the lives of the few people I care about in his hands, I would be his prisoner for as long as he wants me to be.

Damian's POV

"Who the *fuck* is using a jackhammer this time of the morning?" I managed to mumble, not at all loud enough for anyone to hear. Slowly I opened my eyes and looked around the room, with my eyes landing on the door, the sound of water running told me that someone was in this room with me. I stared, waiting for the door to swing open and reveal who was on the other side. Hope secretly crept in as I thought about Leah being the person showering, That somehow I managed to find her and bring her home... to me.

The door swung open and my mind froze. This couldn't be happening. No.

"Morning baby, sleep well? I would be surprised if you didn't after the effort you put in last night." Marisha giggled as she walked out of the bathroom wearing nothing but a towel wrapped around her torso, barely covering her body. My mind didn't seem to be able to comprehend what happened. I didn't even know if anything *had* happened. Marisha started to slink her way over to the bed, a grin that showed just how much of a succubus she was, snuck onto her face and made me cringe. *What did I ever see in her? Sure, she's gorgeous to look at, but once you get to know her she shows you just how ugly she can be.* Shock runs through me as I begin to realise the possibilities of what could have happened last night and the thoughts did nothing to the nausea caused from the hangover.

As Marisha crawled over the bed, trying to get to me I sat upright fast, putting my hands out in front of me to stop her getting any closer. "No." I began, shaking my head at the same time. "No, this can't be happening." She stopped trying to get to me, looking me in the eyes and ran the back of her fingers down my left cheek, "oh sweetie, don't you remember the magic we made?" Her eyes turned to stone with no emotion left in sight as she started pouting at me, "oh, here I was thinking you wouldn't ever be able to forget." She crossed her arms over her chest, her attempt at acting cute just made her look like an evil bitch. I thought about trying to throw the doona off me and make a run for it but that was when I realised I was completely naked. *Holy fuck, she must be right... I fucked this bitch last night and now she will hold it over me forever.* Shivers ran down my spine at the thought of my dick being inside her. "Awwwww, what's the matter baby?" She said, grabbing my chin roughly shaking my head as she did. "You have the morning after regrets?" I grabbed her wrist and yanked her hand away. "Regret doesn't begin to cover it, Marisha. Now, I have to get to the office."

I slid out of the bed and started to dress all the while hoping my keys were here somewhere. I pulled my pants over and up my legs and heard the rattle and I instantly felt a little lighter knowing I would be able to escape.

I turned, heading to the door to make my exit when Marisha spoke again, calling out my name. "Damian!" I hesitantly turned my head to see her smiling, "I'll see you soon." The grin told me she was cooking something up and I definitely wasn't going to enjoy it.

Chapter 24

Leah's POV

I laid on the grass out the back of the house where Mike had taken me to, and felt the soft grass under me mould to my body. I knew I needed to relax my mind before my anxiety would reach new levels. I closed my eyes and focused on the heat from the summer sun as it entered my body, making me feel warm from the outside in.

I felt myself calm down, the vitamin D doing exactly what I wanted it to do.

As I took a deep breath in and held it for a

second, my heart rate started to slow down. Images of Damian danced through my mind. His stunning eyes, his handsome face, that smile that could make any woman's knees weak. A grin slowly crept over my face at the images of Damian but quickly disappeared when someone stepped in the line of sunshine forcing darkness over my body.

I opened my eyes and saw hands coming down towards me grabbing me around the throat as I was lifted up onto my feet. I was held there, his grip around my throat so strong that I struggled to breathe.

I started to grab and pull at his hands, trying to loosen them so I wouldn't struggle so much, ultimately failing as I started to fall into the black abyss that appeared before me. *Death is better than having to deal with this.*

I allowed my eyes to close, begging the darkness to take me. Unfortunately, Mike decided to let go and I finally took a breath.

"Oh no, Leah." I heard him huff, "You don't get to just give up." Mike whispered into my ear, "you don't get to just leave, I am having way too much fun with you." He paused for a moment and I watched as anger flew through his eyes. "Now that you have people you care about, it is making this game more fun!" The grin that started to cover his face was twisted and evil and I could tell he had something planned. "The surprises that I have planned for you, WOW!" He let my throat go and made the brain explosion gesture. " You are going to *love* it!" He shrugged before he continued. "Or not,
Either way *I* will love it!"

I had no idea what he was going to do, but I knew him. I wouldn't have put anything past him.

I wanted to make him stop, stop with this craziness. I

tried that before and all that did was lead me to broken ribs. I just needed him to finally give into his urge and kill me.

"Stop thinking, Leah. You know I hate it when you think..." His tone got aggressive quickly and his hands were around my neck once again. "You know I can't trust you, I wish I could but you made your bed, now you have to lay in it." He squeezed a little tighter, "It is your own fault that I don't." He said through clenched teeth, while his grip got stronger and my ability to breath lessened.

Finally he is going to do it and I will be freed.

He let one of his hands go from around my throat and pulled it back. Last thing I remember is seeing his first come flying towards me, then black....

My eyes fluttered open, and I blinked a few times as I looked around and noticed I wasn't outside anymore.

It was dark and damp, but I was in a room.

I tried to sit up but the pain was too much and I crashed back down to the ground that was beneath me. Sobbing, I tried to pull my hands up to my face so that I could hide my tears, but something held me back, making it so I couldn't lift it.

I lifted my head and looked around, trying to figure out where I was. As I got a glimpse of my surroundings I realised I wasn't in a room, I was in some kind of Cellar.

Panic started to rise with the knowledge I was locked in there with no idea of where I actually was. *How could this happen? Who would do this?*

As the words went through my mind a heavy metal door opened to the side of me allowing a small amount of light in. That's when I saw him... That is when I saw Mike. The smirk that spread across his face disgusted me.

"Mike! Where are we?" I asked, my tone stayed even and

calm as I spoke. I watched him as he stepped closer, the evil that lived inside him owned the room.

"Oh, Leah. I have brought you to a very special place." He sat on the pathetic excuse for a mattress that I was on and grabbed my chin, yanking my head forward to meet his. My lip split instantly with the contact made and all he did was laugh. "Leah, don't look at me like that... I'm not a bad person." He raised his eyebrows like he was waiting for me to respond to his bullshit. We both sat there, the silence lingered between us until he realised he wasn't going to get anything from me.

He stood up fast and turned, slapping me across the face as he did. "Listen to me you pretty little cunt. *I own you!*"

He got right in my face making our foreheads touch, he pointed at me, jabbing me in the chest hard with each word he spoke. His voice was low and gravelly. "You hear me, *bitch?* You are *MINE!*"

He stepped back from me, the anger he felt dripped off him, filling the room. I watched as his chest rose and fell with each breath, he looked like he had run a marathon. I had never pushed him this far before so I had no idea where we were heading.

If only I could see into the future...

Chapter 25

Mikes POV

Most people would think that I went too far with Leah but that bitch needs to learn who is boss, and it sure as fuck ain't her.

I walked up the stairs away from the cellar where I have my 'special guest' living to hear the knock on the front door. *Who the fuck could that be?*

I closed one eye and looked through the peephole. *Shit!*

I swung the door open, stopping the woman from walking into my private space. "What the fuck you doing here?" I said between clenched teeth as I grabbed her by the back of her head and pulled her mouth to mine, kissing her hard. I wrapped some of her hair around my hand and yanked on it forcing her head to Jolt backwards. The bitch moaned loudly as the pain hit her.

"How did you go? Is everything going to plan?" I mumbled as I turned her around so she faced the wall.

"Mmm, yes Sir." She said, the words dripped from her mouth as I used my foot to slide her legs open. I lifted the shirt she had on and pushed the g string to the side, seeing that she was ready to take what I had to give her.

Unzipping my pants, I pulled my dick out and rammed it into her wet hole. It wasn't the hole I wanted my dick in but it would suffice.

As I grabbed her shoulders I started to pound into her hard, even with me holding onto her shoulders her head kept hitting the wall with the amount of force I was using.

I closed my eyes and imagined it was Leah I was fucking.

I imagined her tight cunt being wrapped around my cock, making every time I pulled out feel like heaven. I grabbed one of the tits that swung around with the movements we made and squeezed hard. I pulled on her nipple and my visitor moaned loudly, breaking the illusion I had going. *Fucking slut.* I took my hand from her tit and moved it up to her mouth, covering it with my hand. "Do not make a sound you fucking whore. Nod if you understand." I said aggressively, all the while taking my cock out of her dripping pussy and sliding into her ass. My dick started going soft inside her, I needed to do something to get going again. Once I felt her nod her head I let go of her mouth and slid my hand down to her throat, wrapping my palm around it and gripping it tightly. The moment I heard her breathing change and she struggled a little I started to get hard. I held her even tighter and listened to her breathing. I knew she was starting to panic. Each breath she took was shallow, like it was a struggle to get the little oxygen I allowed her to actually have. Amongst the panic her pussy started to respond by gripping my dick like it wanted me out, but I wasn't going anywhere. In fact, knowing I had her life in my hands made me ridiculously hard and I was in full swing. I didn't care if this bitch died on my dick, I would still cum inside her. Thrusting myself in and out, faster and faster I started to grunt each time I pushed myself all the way inside of her. Between her lack of oxygen and her head hitting the door frame with each thrust I could feel her starting to slip in and out of consciousness and excitement ran through my veins knowing that she soon won't know what is happening. I came right after I felt her slip into unconsciousness, instantly I let her go and watched as she fell onto the porch hitting the concrete with a thud. I smirked and shook my head as I put my dick back in my pants, "fucking amateur." I mumbled as I walked inside and closed the door behind me, leaving the slut passed out on the other side. Best thing about living in the woods is there is no-one to walk by and see her. As I walked to the kitchen I passed the door that led down to Leah and I stopped, listening for any sounds but heard nothing so I kept going.

I grabbed a 6 pack and made my way back to the living room, turning on the tv to watch the bullshit they called entertainment.

I channel surfed and downed beer after beer, trying to forget Leah in the cellar, but eventually I gave in to my urges. I stood and headed down the hall, stopping at the door that led to my one desire.

Turning the chrome worn handle the door slowly creaked open and I walked down the stairs. The smell of the damp earth couldn't overpower the stench of urine. The thought of Leah pissing in a corner of a room entertained me and I let out a little chuckle, but the thought also turned me on and now I had to have her. I had to take Leah, if she liked it or not.

As my feet touched the bottom step I heard her sobbing. Sobbing and whispering that cunt's name. I glared at her, noticing she was asleep. She was asleep and calling for him. *That mother fucking piece of shit.*

I stormed over to her, gripping her hair in my hand before pulling her off the 'bed'. She woke up screaming. "Mike!? Where are you taking me?" She yelled out, her voice letting me know just how scared she truly was, and scared she should have been. I had rage running through my veins and she was my plaything. My toy to use as I pleased, and right now? I was going to do whatever I wanted to her. She was going to get everything I had to give and she was going to take it.

I pulled her up the stairs into the main house and towards the stairs that lead to my bedroom all the while having to listen to her scream.

"Jesus, Leah. Would you just shut up??" I yelled out at her, "You're ruining the mood for fuck sake…" My anger was controlling my every move and I planned to get it all out.

As I walked through the bedroom doorway I threw Leah onto the bed, I stood still, breathing heavy with my fists clenched. I was a predator and this little bitch was my ultimate prey….

Chapter 26

Leah's POV

Being thrown onto the bed by my hair I felt a chunk rip from my scalp causing me to scream out in pain. I opened my eyes and looked up, seeing Mike standing solid in one spot like a beast who was ready to consume what he had caught. His fists were closed so tight his knuckles had turned white and I couldn't help but notice the way his chest rose and fell with every heavy breath he took.

I had been in a constant state of fear but I never like to let it show, right now however, I couldn't stop the terror. It showed all over me. My body shook and tears ran down my face. I wasn't able to control the sobs that escaped, The sound flooded the room and only seemed to get worse the closer Mike walked to me. His face was scrunched up and his eyes looked like they had turned black. He had a look of pure evil and this time I didn't know if I was going to survive the assault. As he stood directly in front of me I craned my head, looking up at him hoping that this wasn't it for me. I wanted to get out of here, I wanted to tell my friends I loved them, I wanted to tell Damian how I felt but I knew none of this was going to happen.

I took a deep breath and slowly released it, accepting the fact that this could be it. I let my head drop and once it hit the bed I felt my tears dry up. Mumbling, "Just do it." I lifted my head once more, speaking louder this time. "Just kill me already, Mike." Out of the corner of my eye I saw him kneel down, his eyes were soft, a contrast of what they just were a minute ago. They didn't stay that way for long before the nastiness came back and he grabbed my hair once more, pulling my head backwards forcing me to look at him. "Oh, baby. I'm not going to kill you." He said as he kissed my lips. "I am however, going to tie you to my bed and fuck you until I have had enough." Grinning as he pulled me backwards by my hair until I collapsed on my back.

He lent over me, grabbing me by my shoulders and held me down. I tried to fight back but he was too strong and my wriggling amounted to nothing except for managing to close my legs. Mike had different ideas and used one of his knees to slide my legs apart. I started swinging my arms around frantically trying with everything I had to get him off me but all that did was earn a bloody lip.... Again. I closed my eyes and turned my head to the side, I had to imagine I was somewhere else. I couldn't be here anymore. I imagined I was in a house. It was noisy out the back so I got up from the couch to go see what was happening. Walking through the sliding door to the backyard I saw Damian but the bbq, tongs in one hand and a drink in the other. He was laughing as he argued with someone about his cooking skills. I watched him as he looked around the yard until his eyes finally locked onto mine. He smiled the kind of smile that melts a woman's heart and I grinned back at him. He started walking towards me. "Look at me Leah. Don't you dare close your eyes and imagine *him*. You will only ever have me running through your pathetic excuse of a brain." Mike's words had pulled me from my dream. I couldn't stop them anymore and I let the tears roll off my face and onto the fabric below me. He grabbed my chin and forced me to look at him as he thrust himself inside me once again. I couldn't fight anymore, I gave up, I laid there underneath him and just let him do as he pleased with my body.

Finally he finished and rolled off of me, collapsing to the side of me. "Well, night then you cunt." He said as he rolled over, making it so he had his back to me grunting at me, "go take a shower, you fucking stink."

I sat up on the side of the bed sobbing. I'm not sure how long I was like that but I noticed Mike had started to snore. Knowing he was asleep made me feel a little safer to jump under the water and wash myself so I got up and stumbled my way towards the bathroom door, spying something on his dresser on my way I stopped and looked. My eyes grew wider as the realisation of what was sitting in front of me hit. I turned and looked back at Mike who was still sound asleep. Reaching out I took the object and quietly walked into the bathroom silently closing the door and locking it behind me. I opened my hands up, looking down at the phone Mike had left lying around. Instantly but with shaking hands I started dialling numbers. I heard the ringing through the earpiece and closed my eyes. *Please answer. I need you... Please...* I begged as I listened. Just before I hung up a groggy voice came through.

"Hello?" I paused, not able to say anything. "Who is this?" I sucked in a breath, "Leah?" I heard hope, for the first time in god knows how long I heard hope in the voice on the other end. "Leah, is that you?" Panic started to come through the phone and I knew I had to answer. I whispered, trying to keep my voice as low as possible so Mike didn't wake up. "H-h-h-hi." I managed to get out from between my chattering teeth. "Maria?" I questioned her, "Leah, my dear, we have been worried sick, where are you?" Worry seeped through the tone she spoke. I started sobbing but still kept my voice low, "Maria, I have to be quick, I have Mike's phone and I'm hiding in the bathroom. He took me. Keep this number but never contact it. If he finds out I've called you he will kill me." I heard her suck in her breath as she came to the realisation I didn't run. Delete this call, Leah. Stay alive, dear. Damian and I will find you. Try and get the phone again when you have more of an idea of where you are. Keep an eye out for any landmarks. We will find you, Leah. Now go before he finds you." The shock still ran through me so I could only manage two words. "Okay, Maria." As I pulled the phone away from my ear I heard her yell out to wait, I pulled it closer to the side of my head when I heard Maria's words. "You are so brave, Leah. I am so proud of you." And the line went dead. *She thinks I'm brave? Pffffft I'm not brave.*

Chapter 27

Damian's POV

Why?

I dropped my head into my hands as I tried to come up with a logical reason why I would get so wasted that I would willingly sleep with Marisha. I shouldn't have gone there again. It's like I want to continuously punish myself. I threw myself backwards and landed against the cushions that lined the couch in my living room.

I closed my eyes and placed my arm over them as I remembered when Leah brought me home the last time I had made this same stupid mistake.

How she looked as I walked into the kitchen standing by the stove as she prepared me food. I brought back the memory of the way she looked at me as she noticed the water running down my body and being caught in the towel that's wrapped around my hips. I pulled at the memory, remembering the way she sucked in her breath as she looked me up and down and the way she bit her bottom lip as if she tried to stifle a moan.

The Memories turned me on and suddenly my dick is testing the strength of the zipper on my jeans. I undid my belt and whipped it out of the hooks on my pants before unclasping the button and pulling the zipper down, freeing my cock of its prison.

It flung out, standing at attention directly in front of me, the memories of Leah proving to me what I didn't want to admit.

I was so angry with myself, I was the reason she ran off with Mike. My mind started to flood with angry thoughts, but my hard on didn't go down.

I grabbed my dick aggressively and started to tug on it. I didn't deserve to enjoy what I did to myself. Pumping my palm up and down my cock as I grabbed hold of my ball sack and twisted, causing so much pain, but at the same time amazing pleasure.

I looked down and was able to imagine Leah's mouth was wrapped around my cock, spit dripping from her mouth as she gagged on my length. I imagined I grabbed her by the throat and squeezed softly, earning a moan from her. I felt the vibration of the sound around my dick and I came hard, my cream hit the couch making a mess on the black leather. *Least it's easy to clean up.*

I sat back letting my now limp dick fall from my hand as I shook my head and

let out a sigh. I had been defeated.

I tried to do the right thing for Leah, I wanted her so bad. So many times I thought about have her up against the full length windows of my office, showing the world either her sexy ass or gorgeous tits as they squashed against the see through panels while I fucked her brains out, but that wasn't meant to be, I took too long. She is off with Mike somewhere and she made it clear she didn't want me to find her... she is worth more than she thinks. You didn't find that kind of pure soul very often and I let it go before I even had it. "You are a fucking idiot," I mumbled to myself.

The ring tone of my phone blasted through the silence, frightening me out of my own thoughts. I sat upright and grabbed it, flipping it over in my hand so I could see the screen.

Caller ID said Maria. *That's weird, what is she doing calling me this time of night?*

I slid the green button across the screen and put the phone to my ear. "Maria?" I questioned before I continued, "what's wrong? Are you okay?" The silence after my questions was deafening and I knew something was up. "Maria!" I commanded, knowing that tone of voice would snap her out of whatever had happened. She cleared her throat, "well, Damian..." she paused again, "Leah called me." The words vomited from her mouth like she didn't want to tell me. She cut short my train of thought as she kept talking, "Leah called me and Mike has taken her.... Like kidnapped. Damian, she's been kidnapped." I was shocked, I couldn't understand what Maria was telling me... "What did you say? Leah's been what?"

Maria spoke slower this time, allowing my brain to comprehend the words she spoke. *Leah was forcibly taken by Mike? He is literally holding her captive.*

I gripped the phone tighter and squeezed my eyes closed. *This entire time he has been doing whatever he pleased with her and she had to take it.* "Where is she, Maria?" I asked, praying she had an answer.

"I don't know Damian. She had no clue where she was either. All she said was that Mike has her and whatever is going on is very very bad. She needs us to find her." My brain was scrambling with its emotions. "Damian, she needs *you* to find her." Leah needed me. "Maria, cancel all my appointments for tomorrow. Do not call me unless it is about Leah." The tone that came out of my mouth was one I had never heard before but it meant business and Maria knew it. "Understood, sir." She said into the phone before hanging up.

Processing what I had just been told, I scrolled through my phone, finding the person I needed to call, before hitting on call and listening to the ringing on the other end.

The phone stopped ringing, "Damian? Bro it's late, why the call?" There was silence for a little bit before I spoke up, "Markus, I need your help. Leah was taken and I have to find her.... I need to find her...." I dropped my head down, "Markus, I think I love her."

Chapter 28

Damian's POV

The silence was deafening as I paced the kitchen floor waiting. Every little sound out the front caught my attention, forcing me to pause in my tracks before I would realise it was nothing and continue on with my pacing.

"Damian, You need to stop." Maria's voice came from behind me, she was always my voice of reason. "It's been a week since she called and you have barely slept." She pointed towards me softly, "look at you, you look exhausted." Her voice was quiet and full of worry.

"Maria, how am I meant to sleep when Leah is out there with that fucking monster having god knows what done to her. I just can't." My body showed my emotions as I let myself fall onto a chair at the dining table. I crossed my arms in front of me and let my head fall forwards in a somewhat uncomfortable but relaxing position as I heard little footsteps come closer to me before stopping. I looked down at Maria's little feet and wondered why she cares about me so much? The thought was gone, replaced by the front door swinging open and Markus making his way through it with someone in tow.

"Damian?" He called out as he walked through the rooms, trying to find me. I didn't have the energy to even answer him, all I managed was a small grunt that Maria wouldn't have even been able to hear.

"We are in here, Markus." Maria called out, letting him know our position in the house. She looked down at me with sadness in her eyes, she knew I was struggling with this and if Markus had shown up here with no answers I would lose my cool.

Markus made his way to us, eyeing me the whole time. I have never felt so vulnerable in my life and it was lucky that it was only these two people who saw it.

Well, these two and this random person that stood to the side of me. I lifted my head slightly to get a look at the imposter in my house.

"Mate, It been a month since Leah called Maria and we have found nothing, Not a fucking thing. This Mike cunt, he's good, I will give him that." Markus paused, allowing me the time to look at him. "But fuck me if we aren't better. This is an associate of mine. He is ridiculously good at finding things that are lost." He pointed to the bloke that was beside him as I eyed him, trying to figure out if he is trustworthy. Markus spoke again. "I know what you are thinking, but man, he is good… like really good. Remember when that woman went to the police and said I had attacked her?" I nodded, that was a fucking ordeal. "Yeah well, Paul here was the one who proved to the cops she was lying through her teeth." My eyes widened at the realisation of who this man actually was and suddenly I had hope.

"Ahhhh, there it is... There is the face." Markus spoke. "You know what is possible now... Don't you?" The sly grin that formed across his face as he spoke only cemented what I was thinking.

"Markus? Are you serious? This is the guy?" My finger pointed through the air towards Paul before running my hands down my face. "Oh my god!" The tone of my voice told him everything he needed to know. I was happy, excited, nervous and so so worried. If this guy blows this and Mike figures out we are looking for them, god knows what will happen to Leah. I took a second to compose myself, *Damian, this man is likely the only chance you will ever have of finding Leah. Look at the positives that can happen, not the negatives!*

I clapped my hands together, "Okay, let's do this!" I stood up quickly, towering over Paul who would have been only five foot ten-ish and my shoulders being double the width of his entire body. He might not be a scary guy to look at, but this man can find every skeleton you would have in your cupboard.You know the stuff you figured would never see the light of day? Yeah, that is what this man could find.... And easily...

I threw my hand out towards Paul, "welcome aboard, Paul." He grinned and pushed his hand forward as he took what I offered and shook it.

"Okay, so.... Where do we start? What do you need from me?" He took his hand out of mine and laughed. "Absolutely nothing." He smirked at me, "Except, of course, the cheque when I return the girl to you."

Chapter 29

Leah's POV

"Hey you little slut!" The words filtered through my sleepy brain as the verbal assault continued. "Get up and shower," I felt a hand wrap around my bicep in my sleepy state and yank me out of the shit that apparently could be classed as my bed, throwing me onto the dirty ground. "you fucking stink. Why would I want to fuck you when you smell like this!?" My eyes flew open to see Mike's fist come down towards my face connecting with my nose.

The force of the punch was so great that my head flew backwards hitting the floor beneath me with a thud. Little speckles started to float around my vision as I tried to focus on Mike. I knew seeing the spots wasn't a good sign and I couldn't let him surprise me like that again. I had to sleep lightly and be aware of everything around me.

I watched as Mike's shoes came closer to me, stopping right in front of me, kicking dust into my face as he did. He slowly bent his knees and crouched down, roughly grabbing my face in his hand before pointing toward me with his free hand, "you... you will do as I *fucking* ask or you will be punished..." his pause along with the look in his eyes made me nervous. "And this isn't the kind of punishment one enjoys... except me!" He yelled out as he threw my face back onto the floor splitting my lip. I kept my eyes closed as I heard his footsteps slowly fade away as he stormed his way out.

It wasn't until I knew he was gone that I allowed myself to cry. I didn't want him to know he broke me. I hadn't had another chance to call Maria and it made me wonder if she had passed on my message... if she had told Damian that I didn't leave because I wanted to.

I sat up slowly and looked around the drab room. The smell had gotten worse than before, but at least now I didn't really notice it. When I scanned along the perimeter I saw that Mike had left the door open for me to shower. A shower means sex, but it also means I could enjoy an everyday comfort that I haven't been able to have. When I am in the shower Mike leaves me alone. It's a time where I can feel the heat from the water. Where I can feel the water as it rains onto my body. Where the soap makes my skin feel like silk and smell like someone who is loved. It's a place where I can forget everything and just be at peace.

I heard a door slam and it broke me from my daydream. As I stood up onto my feet I stumbled over. My body felt so weak from the lack of food and water he had given me and I knew I was slowly dying. I shook my head and got back up, I stood looking at my feet as I curled my toes up and released them. I noticed how boney they looked, Just skin and bone and I knew that the rest of me must have looked the same.

I willed my feet to move and slowly they did. One step, two steps, three steps. I counted my way to the bathroom Mike allowed me to use with his permission. Twenty-three, twenty-four, twenty-five. Twenty-five steps from the doorway to the bathroom and a right turn at step sixteen.

I turned on the water watching as the steam started to fill the room from the heat and the moisture that was created from it started to make me sweat. It Opened up my pores and I felt like the toxicity of this whole situation was being forced out of my body.

I stepped up to the water and put my hand out in front of me, feeling the water temperature before allowing my body to step under it. It was hot, just how I liked it.

I moved my way under the spray and instantly my body relaxed. The pressure was strong and the water was hot, the perfect combination for a makeshift massage as it warmed what little was left of me.

I stood under the spray for what felt like eternity enjoying a little normality. A loud bang broke me from my peace and made me jump. I turned the shower off and stepped out, grabbed the towel and wrapped it around my frame before heading towards the bathroom door and slowly pulling it open.

I could hear a voice, it was muffled but I recognised Mike's voice anywhere and I followed it to the top of the stairs. Mike stood at the bottom pacing as he spoke. I quickly but quietly hid so he couldn't see me but I was able to listen.

"What do you mean he has had someone following you? Why? Why would someone be following you? No-one even knows we know each other!" Mike yelled through the receiver.

I heard him stop pacing and I started to get nervous, *who is he talking to? Who was following them?* Mike's steps started to come up the staircase, one footstep at a time.... Slowly.

I ran back into the bathroom and shut the door, threw my towel over the rail and jumped back in and turned on the water. When Mike barged in I looked like I had been there the whole time, the excess steam was an accident but thank god it was there, it made it believable.

His phone was still up to his ear when I looked at him, a shocked look on my face. "How the *fuck* are you still in here? Get your stupid ass out! You are wasting all my hot water!" Mike shook his head as he walked away mumbling into the phone as he did, but I managed to hear his hurtful words. "Babe, when I'm done with her that cunt won't want her, she will be broken and You and him can live happily ever after in your fucked up rich people world just like you used to."

Wait, what?

Chapter 30

Damian's POV

I listened as Mark waffled on about figures, budgets and schedules. Why we should buy this company and why we should sell this other one. Mark is well respected in this company, he worked here for years, ever since my father started it really and he worked his way up the chain. He knew his stuff and generally I listened hard when he spoke, but today I was bored shitless and I couldn't keep my mind off Leah. I wondered where she was, if she was okay and if my new 'friend' had any news for me.

I snapped to attention when I heard my name being said. I blinked as I looked around the room, noticing everyone's eyes were on me. *Fuck! What did I miss?*

"Ummmm," I moaned. My embarrassment was obvious. I had never been like this before and my lack of focus caught everyone off guard.

"Behind you, Sir." Maria whispered in my ear.

I swung my chair around to see Marisha. My eyes almost rolled out of my head as I turned back to the board and apologised.

"My apologies everyone, Please just give me a second to sort this out. I will be right back." I said, pushing my chair out with my feet, from under the huge meeting desk and walking my way up to Marisha. I grabbed her by the bicep and dragged her out of the boardroom.

"What the fuck are you doing here again, Marisha?" I said as I closed the door behind us. She swung her arm around forcing me to lose my grip on her arm and she stomped her foot like a child.

"I needed to talk to you, Damian, and you haven't answered any of my calls or messages." she turned away from me, the pause making the situation seem more dramatic than it was... *God she loves the drama.*

"Fine. I will meet you after work at the place across the road. Now, fuck off." I was so over her shit. Marisha squealed and bounced on the spot, clapping her hands in excitement. "Oh yay, Damian!" She said with a wink and a smile that I assume was meant to be seductive before she turned and walked down the hall towards the elevator, "See you later, lover." Her high pitched voice bounced off each cubicle making it even more annoying.

I shook my head and dropped it. I looked at my feet and walked back into the boardroom hoping the disruption didn't fuck this deal.

All eyes looked at me as I closed the door behind me. I looked around the room and one by one I saw the mixture of confusion, anger and pity in their eyes. Not wanting the attention on me anymore I pulled my seat out from the table, sat down and spoke, "Did I miss anything important?" I straightened the papers that sat in front of me hoping that everyone in the room gets the hint and gets back to the job at hand.

Mark stared at me, the look on his face was like he was asking if I was okay. *Oh my friend, I am so fucking far from okay.*

"We were just wrapping up, Sir." Maria spoke from next to me, placing a hand on one of mine forcing it to stop fidgeting. "I left some other paperwork that I need you to look over on your desk, it needs to be done asap. After that I can come in and fill you in on what you missed before." I gave her a weak smile as a thank you and tapped her hand, letting her know I appreciate her. I grunted as I stood from the seat, sounding like an old man as I did. I shook everyone's hands before I left the room.

I walked through the office smiling at the staff as I passed them wondering if they had these kinds of problems or if it was just me?

I grabbed the handle on the timber door that led to my office and turned it, letting the door slide along the floor as it opened. The squeaking sounds the hinges made seemed louder than normal and made my brain hurt. I winced at the sound and put my fingers on my temple in hopes that a little pressure would help with the pain but all it did was make it hurt even more.

I slammed my ass onto the couch that sat along the glass wall and dropped my head. *Fucking stress, does it ever stop?* The thought ran through my mind and left again before I could even register that I had a thought at all.

I sat in that office for the rest of the day, not noticing

the day was passing me by at speed and before I knew it, it was time to leave. Excited at the idea of being able to collapse onto my bed and sleep I jumped up and straightened my red button up shirt, the one that Leah very obviously favoured. The memory flashed through my mind. I was leaning with my ass against the conference room table, rolling the sleeves of the red button up shirt up my arm when I glanced her way, her eyes were wide and she was biting her bottom lip, watching each movement I made. A crooked grin appeared on my face as I scoffed at the memory.

She always would watch me, she had no idea I was watching her too. If I had my time again I would have made sure to tell her how I felt, instead I was a stubborn ass who refused to admit he had feelings for this woman. I shook my head forcing myself back into reality and that was when I remembered, *I have to meet Marisha. Fuck!!* I didn't have the energy for any of her bullshit tonight but I told her I would meet her... this one last time.

Chapter 31

Marisha's POV

The people around me stunk like blue collar workers. *Ew.* They all stood so close to each other, too close considering the temperature was still at 29°c at 6pm. The ragged timber flooring made it hard for my stilettos to glide, making me look inexperienced and a fool. The people around me stared as I passed them and words started to fall from my mouth, "what? You've never seen a *real* female before? You used to your street rats?" The disgust was evident in my tone as my lips turned up showing the other people in there how gross they are to me. This place was dull and boring and dirty, Damian knew I hated it and he probably chose it just to frustrate me. A fat old man walked behind me, trying to hold his pathetic excuse for a comb over down. *God I wish Damian would hurry up, this place freaks me out.*

I locked eyes with him, something I instantly regretted, and he gave me a smile. His teeth were yellow, well, what was left of them anyway.

"Marisha, leave the old man alone." Damian's voice broke the thoughts of the teeth in front of me.

I turned my head. Standing in front of me was the man of my dreams. He was tall, solid, handsome and best of all, RICH!

I put on the smile I reserved only for him, the one that used to get me whatever I wanted from him... Then that bitch showed up and I couldn't take what I wanted anymore. The thought made me angry. I wanted his money.

I lent in to kiss him but he pulled away. "Fuck off Marisha. Don't put on a show for the tabloids." He knew me too well, I just needed them to think we were back together. Well, what I am about to tell him may just make that a reality.

Damian's POV

I stood in the doorway watching my psycho ex show her true colours. The way she looked at another human being was disgusting and I couldn't wait to get this little pow wow over with so she could get out of my life forever.

The look in her eyes told me she was on the brink of allowing her 'real' self out and this poor old man didn't deserve that, he just wanted to eyeball something beautiful so he could think about it later while he played with himself.

"Marisha, leave the old man alone." I sighed at her. I started to walk towards her but with my long stride it ended up being only a few steps. Marisha undressed me with her eyes before flashing me her smile, that doesn't work on me anymore, *bitch*. She lent in trying to kiss me but I pulled away. *She has seen the media outside, great.* "Fuck off, Marisha. Don't put on a show for the tabloids." I knew what she was up to and I could bet my fortune she was the one who gave them the heads up that I would be here.

The smirk that slowly appeared on her face was unsettling and one that I had never seen before.

I needed to say something, I needed to distract her from whatever she was planning in that evil little brain. "Ok. I'm here. Say what you have to say and leave." I kept my voice cold and calm. I didn't want her thinking she had any sort of control over me anymore. Her eyes locked onto mine, forcing them to stay there like she had some sort of invisible gravity pull.

"Can we please go somewhere a little more..." she paused as she looked around her again, pulling faces at the other patrons like they were cockroaches. "Private?" She finished. "HA! You have got to be kidding me right? Marisha, you are crazy." I lent forward over the small table that divided us and got close to her, whispering loudly so she would hear over all the noise. "I know you, Marisha. I know you are a slimy scheming bitch.

If we went somewhere more 'private' who knows what you would tell people what happened." I moved back, sitting on the barstool properly again. I motioned to her to move this along, "can we get this over with please, I've got things to do, people to see."

Her arms crossed over her chest making her breasts fall out of the top of her dress even more than they already were. *Can't deny the woman, she does have impeccable tits.*

Marisha grunted. knowing I wouldn't take her shit tonight she started talking.

"Well, like, you know a little while ago when we fucked all night long in that hotel room down town?" She licked her over the top noticed lips trying to be sexy. I couldn't help but roll my eyes at her, her desperation was disgusting.

I pulled her up before she managed to spout any more nonsense. "Actually Marisha I don't. All I remember is waking up hungover as fuck with you coming out of the shower and *telling* me we fucked all night long. There is a difference between our 2 versions of what happened."

The smile slowly started to fade from her face as I started to get one.

I was so zoned into this conversation I hadn't realised my phone had been ringing until another patron tapped me on my shoulder. I looked at him with a raised eyebrow. "Hey!" My tone was happy like him and I were old friends. He raised his glass to me as he slurred, "bro... your phone has been going off non stop. Somebody wants you real bad. Probably the missus seeing where you are." He stopped to wink a drunken wink and pointed to Marisha, "but we know you are with the side bitch, huh?" The laughing that came out of my mouth was loud as I threw my head back. "Classic, thanks for the heads up, man." I shook my head still laughing as I whispered, "side bitch haha"

This time I heard the phone and I was still chuckling as I answered it, "Caldwell."

The voice on the other end stopped me from smiling instantly. "Mr Caldwell, I found him." My eyes popped with the news,

"I'll report back when I have more information." And with that he was gone. I stood up fast and went to walk out but Marisha grabbed my arm. "Damian!" She called as I flung her arm off and turned to face her. "You can't leave yet, I haven't told you yet." Frustrated with her nonsense I tried to leave again, this time making it a few steps away before I heard her voice behind me.... *"I'm pregnant!"* The words shook me but she didn't stop talking, "I'm pregnant and it's yours. We can be a family." I faced her. I was angry. *It's not supposed to be like this, not with her.*

CHAPTER 32

Damian's POV

My nerves showed as I paced the floor of the safehouse. I wondered if Paul had done enough surveillance on Mike, *is a month long enough to know someone's daily movements?*

Paul had seen Leah on several occasions over the month, and noticed how unwell she looked as well as providing photos for me to be able to see for myself. *Big mistake.* All that did was piss me off. I wanted to kill that cunt. No-one should treat a woman like that.

And this is why I am here, pacing the floor of the safehouse. I wasn't allowed to go get Leah.

I was being held hostage by Maria, who in all honesty probably scared me more than any person I had ever dealt with. I had been in meetings with the heads of mafias, gangs and hitmen, but Maria? She terrified me. I heard a noise outside the window, making me stop pacing and look in the direction the sound came from.

I noticed headlights heading towards the house. *It has to be them. It has to be Leah.*

I was frozen. My body couldn't move. I willed it to head towards the door but it stood still. I was so scared that something had happened to Leah that I couldn't bring myself to run out the door and find out.

The handle on the old beaten door jiggled. I heard Markus call out, "Damian! Let us in, quick!" His voice was urgent with a hint of pleading. Before I could even think about his words Maria had jumped up, running over to the door and flinging it open. I watched her as her hands flew towards her face and covered her mouth. *This is it, this is the moment of truth.*

I squeezed my eyes shut, too scared to see if Leah was with them, then I heard it... I heard my name in that sweet tone that I instantly knew belonged to Leah.

My eyes flew open and my legs started to move, I headed towards the front door. I was going to run but the door was only a few strides away from me. Stopping behind Maria my eyes welled up. I stood and stared at Leah, not moving a muscle, just soaking in her appearance. She was beaten, bloody, bruised and skinny.

My anger started to rise the more I looked at her. The more evidence of abuse I saw the more I started to clench my jaw, anger flowing out of my veins and thickening the air around us making everyone uncomfortable.

I grabbed Leah carefully out of Markus' arms and held her close, allowing her to wrap her arms weakly around my neck as I walked us over to a couch. As I laid her down I made sure she was protected by a wall of cushions and comfortable. I knelt there for a minute just watching her chest rise and fall, looking her over closer I noticed her wince with each breath she took.

Seeing her in pain, pain that was caused by Mike made my anger spike. I stood fast and stormed towards Markus and Paul.

"Where is he?" I said, grabbing Markus' shirt and bundling it into my fist, pulling him closer to me.

Markus ripped his shirt from my hand and stepped back, "He... He," He paused and looked away, "he got away, man. I'm sorry." He stood still but tall, not able to look me in the eye but still showing strength, although I could feel his nervous energy flowing from his body as I watched his hands ball into fists as if he was ready to fight me.

It made me soften, *This was my best friend. He wasn't the one I wanted to take out.*

I pulled him into me embracing him. "Thank you." I said loud enough for only him to hear, "Thank you for getting her back to me." I felt his body relax as I said the words, like he had been expecting me to be speaking something completely different and I didn't blame him for that.

Markus wrapped his arms around me, clapping me on the back as he said the words I needed to hear, "Always man, I got your back. We will get your girl fixed up and once she doesn't need us focusing on her *then* we will find that fucking cunt and put him in the ground." I stepped back from him so I could look him directly in the eyes. "I promise you, I will fucking kill him for what he has done to her. He's fucking *DEAD!*"

Maria's voice floated into the conversation. "Damian, we really need to get her to a hospital. She needs a doctor, right now." I looked over at her and nodded, "alright, let's get her into my car." Facing Markus and Paul, "You guys did good, go clean up. Paul, ring me when you are ready and we will sort out your payment." Paul nodded, "Got it boss, now get your girl to a hospital."

I slapped his shoulder before I turned and walked back over to the couch Leah laid on. I bent down, kissing her on the forehead gently before wrapping my arms around her and lifting her up. Maria held the front door open waiting for us to walk through it before she ran off to the car, opening the backdoor and shutting it behind us. I watched her as she ran around the front of the SUV and jumped into the driver's seat and turned the key, starting the car and taking off towards the hospital.

I looked into my lap, watching Leah's swollen and bruised face twitch and I couldn't help it but to lift her hand up to my lips and kiss it softly, whispering into it, "You are safe now, Leah. You are safe with me, I won't let anyone near you again." I don't know if it was coincidence or if she actually heard me but at that moment it felt like her body relaxed so much it melted around my legs and the feeling made me smile, just a tiny bit.

CHAPTER 33

Damian's POV

Knock knock...

Right on time.... The door opened slowly and a head popped into view. "Hi Mr Caldwell. How's our girl today?" She smiled kindly as she walked towards the side of the bed that had all the equipment. "Hey, Rach." I said as I looked up at her from the chair I have become acquainted with and returned her smile. "I think she's doing better, she has had moments where her eyes fluttered like they were going to open but couldn't quite get there." She nodded her head as she listened and did Leah's OBS. "She is such a strong woman, Mr. Caldwell, you must be so proud of her." I looked at Leah and leant over, grabbing her hand in mine, holding it tightly.

"I am." I swallowed hard, "I just wish she would open her eyes so I could tell her." Still holding her hand, I moved it up to my lips, kissing the back of it softly. As I moved our clasped hands back down and rested them on the bed, I stared at this beautiful woman and prayed I got to see those gorgeous eyes looking back into mine once again.

Resting my head on the side of the bed and looking over at Leah, I barely even noticed that the nurse had left the room leaving the two of us alone in the silence again.

She looked so peaceful, even with all the bruises and open wounds you could see she knew she was safe and in turn, relaxed.

With the silence killing me I let go of Leah's hand and stood up, turning around and reaching out for the bluetooth speaker

Maria had bought in. I connected my phone to it and opened up Spotify, scrolling through my playlist until I found the song I was looking for.

Pressing play I played with the volume until I got it sitting perfectly for background music. I sat down on the bed next to her and grabbed her hand and just looked at her as I listened to the words.

'I turn the world over in search of
The story that only you can complete
Even if I lose everything, you are all I need
All of the lights are out here
Hug me

If I close my eyes, it rushes in soundlessly
You pile up in full again in my heart
I don't need anybody but you
I'm not done until the day you come back to my side.'

I need you to come back to me Leah.

I gently moved my free hand to her forehead, sweeping some of her hair aside and behind her ear.

"Leah, I don't know if you can hear me, but I need you to fight, I need you to come back...." I sighed then spoke the words I had been scared to say to her. "To me, I need you to come back to me. I love you, Leah."

Leah's POV

I Heard the music start and I listened to see what it was. After a few seconds I recognised the tune. *Oh! Way back home? I love this song!*

As I hummed along to it in my head I could hear Damian start to speak. "Leah, I don't know if you can hear me, but I need you to fight, I need you to come back...." There was a short pause between his words and finished off with a sigh before he kept speaking. "To me, I need you to come back to me. I love you,

Leah."

I felt someone touch my forehead. It felt soft and warm as it glided across my skin and leaving goosebumps in its wake.

I felt the warmth of the touch as it flowed through my body, making me feel like it was finally waking up.

My eyes fluttered open and closed, I fought so hard to open them and eventually won. My vision was blurry but quickly righted itself. I was laying in the bed staring up only to see Damian's gentle and loving eyes staring back at me. A smile spread across his face as he realised what was happening.

"Hi." One word, all the things I wanted to say to him and I say hi, I shut my eyes and squeezed them tight with embarrassment. My voice was gravelly and dry and It was painful to talk so I decided to just leave it at hi.

"Leah?" My name falling out of his mouth like that made me feel like I was special, like I was the only person alive. I opened my eyes slightly, just enough to see his handsome face looking down at me seriously. I could tell he had something he wanted to say but he just sat silently, staring down at me. There was pain in his eyes and I knew what was on his mind.

I reached over, placing my palm on his cheek and feeling his baby smooth face. "I know." I mumbled as loud as I could muster as I gave him a weak smile. The pain he felt was for the girl he knew before. After everything he did to save me, how could I tell him that she was gone forever?

CHAPTER 34

Leah's POV

The three weeks since being released from the hospital had been a whirlwind. Not having any place to call home but still needing care, Maria offered to take me in, caring for me like the mother I had always prayed for. She had been a godsend when I needed one the most and I was forever grateful to her for that. Damian hadn't come around much to visit me, but he called every day, sometimes multiple times just to check in on me. He was weird with me now, like the reality of what I went through and how damaged I am had finally sunk in.

He couldn't look at me. I disgusted him now and that upset me. I had obviously had too many good things going on and needed to have some bad to bring me down to earth. I should have known, I can't have any good and when I do I get punished.

I looked down at the blanket Maria had draped over my legs earlier as I moved it between my fingers, letting the soft Woollen textures relieve some of my anxieties.

I sighed as I allowed my head to drop, putting my neck in an awkward and uncomfortable position but somehow still relaxing.

Breathe in…. And out…. As I sat relaxed in my chair, focusing on my breathing I heard a noise outside and jumped, my slowed down heart rate now racing again.

I instantly fell to the floor and crawled towards the front door making sure it was locked. I peeped around the corner from the loungeroom noticing the door handle moving. *Someone was trying to get in.*

I refused to let Mike take me again so I stood and hid in the corner of the room between two bookcases with a heavy book in my hands, ready to use as a weapon.

The door squeaked as it opened and the sound of footsteps followed. I listened as the echo of steps came closer until they were almost on top of me.

I stepped out from my hiding spot, swinging my weapon at the intruder, I heard a thud as the book hit its target.

"Ow!" The deep voice mumbled as the book was ripped from my hands. "Jesus, Leah." I looked up and saw Damian rubbing one of his pecs.

I gasped and my mouth fell open as I threw my hands over it before spouting out a million apologies.

"Oh my god, Damian, I'm so sorry. I thought you were someone trying to break in."

Damian placed one of his hands over mine, pulling them away from my mouth, feeling how much they shook, his face showing me clearly how much that worried him.

"I'm sorry, Leah. I should have announced myself. I didn't mean to frighten you, I wasn't thinking."

I lifted my head so I could look at his eyes, but instead I noticed the bags under his eyes.

"You look tired. Have you been sleeping?" My soft voice seemed loud in the quiet that surrounded us.

He gave me a small grin, "I've been busy, lot's of things to do as the CEO." He said, raising his hand and placing it under my chin and gently holding it in place. His gesture was sweet and his touch warmed my heart, it distracted me but not enough to miss the sad look he held in his eyes.

"What's happened Damian?" I sighed as I let Damians hand hold the weight of my head.

"Nothing you need to worry about, Leah."

I didn't believe him still but I knew if he didn't want to tell me there was no way I would be able to get him to say it out loud.

All I was able to do was nod, acknowledging his words, but the look on my face would have told him how I felt.

"Seriously, Leah. It's nothing. You don't have to worry about me." He said letting my face go and wrapping his arms around me.

Instantly I felt at home, his muscular chest radiating the warmth and safety I hadn't realised I desperately needed.

I pulled myself into him tighter and exhaled, feeling all the anxiety and fear that had been running through my veins for weeks, just melt away.

After standing there in our embrace I felt Damian start to pull away. I held him trying to stop him from leaving. "Leah, it's okay, I'm not going anywhere."

Placing his fingers under my chin and lifting my head made me look up at him once again.

His beautiful green eyes flicked between mine as he bent his neck. I closed my eyes, waiting for his lips to finally touch mine again only to be surprised when I felt them on my forehead.

I pulled back, looking up at him once more. "I'm, I'm sorry...." I stuttered, slightly embarrassed at my presumption. "I thought you were going to kiss me." I said, looking at my feet as my cheeks turned bright red.

Damian grabbed my chin and forced my eyes to focus on his, "As much as I would love to take you here against this wall, Leah, I will wait until you are ready for me." The words fell from his mouth like he was making a promise, keeping me safe and seducing me all at once and I was one hundred percent here for it. He was the only one who could make me forget about what I had been through. He made it so I could be free from what Mike had done to me, even just for a little while and it was bliss.

"What if I said I wanted you to do exactly that, Mr Caldwell?" I watched his tongue run over his lips slowly and I knew he was holding himself back from doing exactly what he said he wanted to.

He growled at me, although it sounded more like a tiger than anything else. The sound turned me on and the feeling in my panties let me know just how much.

CHAPTER 35

Damian's POV

What is she saying right now?

I had to process the words she spoke, over and over in my mind before what she had said sunk in.

I heard the sound coming from within my chest before I had realised I was even doing it. The beast inside wanted to take her finally, but the gentleman in me wanted to wait a little longer.

She was staring up at me, my fingers still under her chin. She was begging me with her eyes to take her right here, right now. My hand slowly fanned out and slipped down from her chin to her neck, wrapping around it tightly, but not too tight. I pushed her backwards until her back was against the wall and I leaned down and whispered in her ear, "Let me know if you don't feel comfortable, Leah and I will stop, Okay?" I looked her in the eyes as I watched her nod. "Not good enough Nabi, I need you to say the words. I need to hear you say, yes Daddy."

Leah looked at me, confusion written on her face. "Nabi?" She questioned. "What does that mean?" I smiled down at her, "It means butterfly, and it suits you perfectly." I bent down, gently kissing her lips. "What do you mean?" Her big beautiful eyes were opened wide as she tried to put the pieces together. I grinned, "you have evolved so much. You were in your cocoon for so long and now as you enter my world you have become my butterfly. You have every reason to be bitter and hate the world but you still see the good in it. You *are* the butterfly, Leah."

I watched her, waiting for a reaction that never came. Her lips pulled apart as she spoke, "Damian?" The way she said my name made me feel weird, like something I had never felt before. "Hmm" I said in return.

"Say it again." Now it was my turn to be confused. "Say what?" She smiled up at me. "That you need me to say the words."

Instantly I remembered what we had been talking about. "Oh." I smirked, "Nabi, if you get uncomfortable at any point, you have to tell me, okay? Don't just nod, You have to say the words out loud, I need to hear you say, *Yes Daddy*."

I watched her suck in her breath and cross her legs as she heard me say Daddy. I grinned, "you like Daddy, huh?" I leaned closer, my hand still gripping her neck as my free hand slid its way down the waistband of her pants and finally touching her clit. "Oh you like it, I can feel exactly how much you like it."

Rubbing her clit slowly in circles as I spoke, I could feel the effect I was having on her and knowing that I alone was responsible for her feeling such pleasure made me hard.

I lent my hips forward, allowing my cock, which was now tenting in my pants, to push into her gently. I wanted her to know how easily she could turn me on. The sounds she started making were incredible and I was fighting my urges to squeeze her throat harder, instead I slipped one of my fingers inside her. I felt her pussy tighten around it. I was fighting hard but I felt myself losing the battle. I placed my forehead next hers on the wall and whispering, "Oh fuck Nabi, you are so wet for me." The sounds that came from below us as I moved my finger in and out of her hole were becoming to much. "Fuck it is such a turn on listening to how your body reacts to my touch." I slipped a second finger in which made a valley between them for her juices to run down and drip off the bottom of my hand. "God, Im so fucking hard for you right now, Leah." I have to stop myself, this is about her right now, I need to take it slow.

I stopped, still with my head against the wall beside Leah. My breathing was heavy and I squeezed my eyes closed. I slid my fingers out of the one place I wanted any part of me to be.

The noise Leah made was one of surprise and disappointment and as I looked at her face I could see the sadness, the disappointment but worst of all, the rejection. I smirked, she was so far from the truth with that one and I wanted her to know just how far. I lifted my hand out of her pants and held it between us, letting her see her juices glistening on my hand.

My movement was slow and her eyes followed the whole way as I opened my mouth and put those two special fingers in my mouth before closing my lips around them.

I groaned as the taste of her hit my tongue. She was sweet, like nothing I had ever had before and I wanted more.

"Mmm, Leah." I looked her dead in the eyes, "Have you ever tasted yourself?" I saw her cheeks go pink as she shook her head no. "Oh, Nabi, you are missing out on something amazing." I purred? I watched closely as her mouth parted slightly and she caught her breath.

I raised an eyebrow, "Would you like to try?" I asked her. She looked away for just a moment before looking at me again and giving me a small nod and a cheeky smile. "Yes, Daddy." She drawled, her tone soft and sultry.

"Leah, hearing you call me Daddy, is by far the sexiest thing I have ever heard, and I am not going to take you right here. I am going to take my time with you, Leah. You will know what you taste like after I have had my feed first…"

I threw an arm around Leah's chest and my other under her legs and picked her up. I felt her wrap her arms around my neck and grip my hair. Hard.

"Baby, you keep doing things like that and I won't be able to focus only on you."

Leah grinned at me, "I want to focus on you, Daddy."

I walked towards a bedroom, any bedroom, with all intentions to make this woman cum like she's never cum before.

CHAPTER 36

Leah's POV

My mind was racing. I had so many things running through it. So many scenarios of what would happen... what *could* happen.

My anxiety had skyrocketed and somehow, like he could feel it, Damian glanced down as he carried me towards the room.

Noticing me already looking at his handsome face, he bent down and gently brushed his lips over mine and my worries faded into nothingness and I knew I would be safe, that Damian wouldn't do anything I didn't want to do.

I wrapped my arms around his neck and pulled him in tighter and opened my mouth, allowing him all the access he desired and being the greedy man I knew he could be, he took my offer. I felt his tongue run over my lips before entering my mouth.

His kisses deepened, and became heavy and possessive, claiming what he knew was his. I started to kiss him back, my tongue entered his mouth and collided with his.

The passion between us got stronger by the second and the urgency to have him inside me had become indescribable. I had never been like this before.

I heard a door creak open. Damian pulled his mouth away from mine, and I opened my eyes, looking at his. There was a fire in them, a primal need. His inner animal was slowly taking over.

He threw me onto the bed and I bounced backwards sitting perfectly in the middle of the bed.

I bit my bottom lip, wondering what he was going to do to me next. My eyes never left him as he undid the cufflinks in the arms of his shirt and one by one slowly rolled them up his arms, exposing all his tattoos. That sight alone made me wet. I could feel how bad I needed to change my panties.

Damian undone the top few buttons on his shirt allowing me to have a peek at the tattoos he had on his chest before he looked at me and smirked, running his eyes down my body like he was undressing me with them and I couldn't stop the small moan that escaped my lips.

He stepped forward until his legs were against the foot of the bed, his gaze intensified with every passing second.

He sucked his bottom lip between his teeth then grinned again, "oh, Nabi. I plan on absolutely devouring you tonight." He pulled up his knees one at a time and placed them on the mattress and slowly crawled forward before coming to a stop at my feet.

Damian placed a hand on each of my feet, fanning his fingers over the tops and started to run his fingers from the tips of my toes to my shins, only stopping because I flinched as his hand slid over a spot that was still healing.

"I'm sorry, Did I hurt you?" Damian's question came out as a rush of words as panic spread across his face and he pulled his hands away from me.

I quickly sat up and grabbed his hands, pulling them towards me. "No, no. You didn't hurt me." I gave him a small but genuine smile, but then the memories came flooding back and the smile disappeared and I looked away letting go of his hands. "It was from..." I paused, trying my hardest to say the words but in the end, failing and only being able to whisper, "before."

Damian crawled up the bed, sitting back on his ankles. He sat so close to my body I felt his warm breath on my neck. The quiet between us wasn't uncomfortable but after a second of fighting the tears Damian placed his fingers under my chin, turning my head so I faced his. The gesture from him was so simple, but held so much worth.

This man was worth more than his weight in gold. The size of his heart knew no bounds and right now it was all focused on me.

"I'm sorry, Leah." He whispered, running his thumb over my lips. "I'm sorry you went through all that shit, and if you don't want to do anything we don't have too." He pulled my chin up further so our noses were almost touching. "I just want to have you in my arms where I know you are safe."

I reached up, running the palm of my hand down his face before I pulled him forward, smashing our lips together and instantly we had both forgotten about what had happened in the past.

Damian started pushing forward as our lips stayed connected, silently telling me he wanted me to lay back.

Following his lead, I did as he silently requested feeling my back hit the mattress.

His huge body moved over the top of me and I opened my legs wider to accommodate him allowing him to move himself between them.

He rested himself on top of me and I could feel how much he wanted me, his cock rubbed up my stomach with every move he made.

The feeling made me lose my breath, and Damian had to remind me what I needed to do. He pulled his lips back from mine and lowered them to my left ear, nibbling it then whispered, "Breath, Nabi." His tone was sexy and soft but demanding and powerful.

"Leah," He moaned into my ear again, "Sit, Leah." His words were a command not a question and I did as I was told.

Sitting up in front of Damian as he scanned my body with his sexy eyes, I couldn't help but think about what he saw in me. I'm me, nothing special, why me?

My thoughts didn't make it much further as I felt his hands around my waist, slowly lifting my shirt up and eventually over my head, throwing it to one side of the room.

He grabbed my breasts, squeezing them ever so slightly as he moved towards the nipples, which were hard and ready for some attention from him.

His fingers stopped close to where I wanted them… No, Needed them, but didn't make it all the way, leaving my nipples aching for his touch.

He didn't disappoint when his lips came down on them one by one, licking, sucking and flicking them with his tongue.

I was running on pure instinct, running my fingers through his hair before clutching it all in my hands and moaning loudly as I slowly started to grind myself on him.

I reached my hand down between us, trying to touch his cock but Damian stopped me going for what I wanted and pulled my hand back behind my head and held it there.

He growled at me, "No, Leah. Tonight is about you, sweetheart."

He ran his fingers over the top of my now saturated panties, gliding over my clit lightly making me moan once more.

"Your panties are in the way, Leah. Remove them." He demanded. I pulled my ass off the bed, allowing Damian to pull my underwear off and showing him the sight he obviously wanted to see.

Damian sucked his bottom lip between his teeth and growled. "God, Nabi. Look at you glistening for me." I watched as he laid down between my legs and his tongue licked my clit once. He looked up at me, a smirk on his face as well as my juices. "MMMm, you taste so sweet. You are my new favourite flavour, Leah." He grunted before he bent back down between my legs, taking my clit into his mouth and sucking hard.

Damian slowly let it slide out of his mouth still sucking a little and the vibrations of his groans as he did, giving me a feeling I hadn't had before.

Damian's mouth left my body and it was then I noticed the wet patch under my bum. Absolutely mortified I had pissed myself I tried to sit up. Damian stopped me, placing his hand on my shoulder. "What do you think you are doing, Leah?" To me Damian's voice was full of his disappointment and I covered my face, I was so embarrassed. I felt like I was about to cry, I wouldn't be able to handle the rejection Damian was about to give me because of what I had just done.

Damian grabbed my hands and gently pulled them away from my face and took hold of my chin pulling it upwards so he could see me clearly.

"Hey hey hey." He said softly, his worry seeping through his words. "What's going on? What happened just now?"

His soft voice was still gruff but powerful as well as caring. "I… I made a mess, I'm sorry." I tried to hang my head but his grip on my chin wouldn't allow it, instead I watched as anger flashed through his eyes. "Leah, you didn't make a mess, you were enjoying what I was doing to you… That isn't anything to be sorry for."

Damian lent down, kissing my forehead, as he pulled back he stopped just in front of my face gently kissing my lips with his. "How about we just lay together tonight, yeah?"

I nodded, feeling like I was free to say no and he wouldn't force me to do what he wanted. "Ah, Leah?" He questioned.

I gave him a small weak grin in response. "I just want you to know… I'm not him. I am nothing like him and I don't care how long it takes or what I have to do to prove it to you, I will wait for you to realise it. I've got your back, Nabi"

This man was the absolute sweetest thing on the planet.

CHAPTER 37

Damian's POV

I got carried away, I pushed her too far, I was so into what I was doing I forgot what happened to her. I needed to remember to keep the tone of my voice soft, non threatening. I can't have her thinking she's doing something wrong when she's not. I'm an absolute idiot.

I had laid next to Leah all night, just holding her, watching her. She looked at ease, finally looked like the old Leah, the one from before, the one whose smiles would light up a room.

The images of a happy Leah ran through my mind, making me grin.

"What are you thinking about?" Leah's voice broke through the silence, bringing me back to reality. I lowered my eyes, looking down at her. I smiled more and lifted my hand, running it along her face pushing some stray hair behind her ear. "You..." I stopped and waited for a response, when I didn't get one I continued. "Your smile. I was thinking about your smile, Leah." I watched as she processed what I had said, knowing the exact moment it clicked in her head that I was thinking about her.

She bit her lip and looked away, not in the way you do when you are flirting, but more in the shy girl-next-door way.

This beautiful woman didn't believe she was worth anything or that anyone would want her... anyone would *choose* her. I was going to have to show her just how wrong she was.

With my morning gruff tone still in effect, I spoke, "Leah." The soft demand made her look at me once again with wide innocent eyes. "Leah, can I kiss you?" I asked her. I'm not normally one to ask for what I want but she is different, I didn't want to be too intense and scare her off.

I watched as she thought about my question. I could see the conflict she was having within herself. Just as I was about to speak up, letting her know it was okay to say no she rushed forward crashing her lips onto mine. The shock of what happened passed through me quickly and I started kissing her back, matching her energy so I didn't scare her again. I ran my tongue over her lips, asking for permission to enter, permission she gave to me.

I followed her lead as she started moving, laying on her back. I crawled over the top of her, finding my place between her beautiful thick thighs.

Pulling my face away from hers slightly, I asked, "Is this okay?" I asked her permission, making sure she was okay with me putting myself there. Leah nodded her head and I went straight back to her lips kissing them with passion beyond anything I had ever felt.

Leah's ran her arms under mine and wrapped them around my body, allowing her to be able to grip my skin with her fingertips, squeezing them hard enough that her nails broke the skin and drew blood. She had no idea what she was doing to me and how hard I was working to hold it together so I didn't scare her again.

I had my forearms resting on either side of her head as I pulled some of the sheets into my hands, clutching them, hoping it would help keep me in control.

Leah pulled her face back from mine a little and she spoke, "Damian, I want you..." I stopped everything, looking at her, my eyes never leaving hers.

"Damian? Did you hear me?" She asked. "I want you to fuck me." She didn't ask. It was a demand. Normally a demand like this would come with punishment, but she isn't anywhere near ready for anything like that, and I don't want her to feel like her choices are being taken out of her hands.

I smashed my lips down onto hers, the kissing became intense and passionate.

Leah moaned quietly, the sound turned me on more than anything I could ever imagine.

I started grinding my cock against her as we kissed, feeling how turned on she was through the fabric of her panties and my boxers.

Her juices were coating my boxers and I wasn't even inside her yet. I moved my lips across her face, nibbling on her ear before kissing my way down her neck and stopping at her collarbone. I licked across the outline of the bone, taking in her scent as I did. I slid a hand up her shirt slowly, allowing her the opportunity to tell me to stop... she didn't so I kept going, raising my hand closer and closer to her breast before I felt it in my palm. I softly squeezed it as I found the nipple and gripped it between my fingers and gently pulled on it. Instantly it went hard. I needed to taste her... Now.

"Sit up Leah, I want to see you." She did as I commanded without hesitation. She looked me right in the eyes as she moved, you could see the lust dancing through them. *She wants this as much as I do.*

Leah lifted her arms as I clutched at the bottom of the shirt she had slept in, pulling it up over her chest, I exposed her perfect breasts.

I paused for a second, just to appreciate what I was about to concour.

Leah's body was unreal. Without a bra her tits sagged a little. They weren't like any of the other women I had been with, big perky and fake. They were beautiful and natural.

I heard Leah clear her throat and I knew my staring had started to make her feel uncomfortable.

I pulled the shirt over her head and arms and tossed it onto the other side of the room.

I dipped my head down, capturing one of her nipples in my mouth as I massaged the other with my hand.

Pulling back just a little I licked the tip of her nipple then slyly looked up, barely moving my head from its position.

"Has anyone ever told you how perfect your tits are, Leah?" The look on her face told me the words I had spoken took her by surprise. "You don't even understand how beautiful you really are." I mumbled before softly guiding her backwards until her spine was safely on the mattress.

I didn't know how much longer I could keep myself from fucking her. I felt this urge to take her, to have her, but instead I slid myself down over her body, kissing a pathway to the one place I desired the most.

Laying on the bed in only her drenched panties and me between her thighs, I couldn't stop myself from pulling aside the material and licking up some of her juices.

She tasted nothing like I had ever tasted before and without thinking I dove back in, her juices spreading across my face. I felt her as she grabbed fistfuls of my hair and pulled me even closer to her.

My tongue made its way into her pussy. I started to fuck her with it.

I was fucking, licking and sucking her, lost in my own world of pleasure, and completely unaware of the impact I actually had on this woman. My mind was focused solely on the task at hand and it wasn't until I felt my face get drenched in liquid did I realise that Leah had squirted all over me.

"Nabi?" She looked up at me and watched me closely as I wiped the mess from my face with my fingers before putting them all in my mouth one by one, slowly licking her offering off each of them. "You taste delicious, beautiful..." she watched me through her eyelashes and I could sense she was curious. Offering one of my fingers, she grabbed it and wrapped her tongue around it pulling it into her mouth.

Leah lowered her arm, her palm making contact with my dick through my boxers and slowly started to slide it up and down my shaft.

I threw my head back with pleasure, groaning as I did. "Fuck, Leah." I bit my lip as I started to move my body along with her hand. I closed my eyes but I could still see her in my mind. The look she had in her eyes when she first moved her hand between us. She was starting to enjoy herself.

Leah stopped moving, the sudden lack of movement bringing me back to earth. My eyes flew open, worried something had happened only to see Leah lick her palm as she stared me in the eyes and placed her hand between the elastic of my boxers.

I didn't want to seem forceful, but I wanted her to also know how much I wanted to make her mine.

"Leah?" I paused, staring into her beautiful eyes. "Be careful Nabi, sometimes I bite." I smirked at her as her hand slid under my boxers and grabbed my dick.

The soft skin of the palm of her hand gently rubbed the sensitive skin. Leah kept eye contact with me while she worked me. "Oh Daddy, I *want* you to bite. I want everyone to see I am yours."

That was all I needed to hear from her. I pulled my boxers off and threw them away, and bent back down, once again placing myself between Leah's legs.

I could feel the opening of her pussy on the tip of my cock, she was wet and waiting for me and I didn't want to waste any more time.

"Nabi, are you ready to take Daddy's big dick in your tight little pussy? Hmm?" Leah nodded, the smile on her face let me know she was ready.

Leah's POV

I felt like I should have been nervous, but as Damian looked into my eyes I just felt safe. Safe and at home. This was meant to be. This was meant to happen with this man. Damian is the one who was meant to save me from the life I survived for so long.

"Nabi, Are you ready to take Daddy's big cock? Hmm?"

Damian's words excited me. I could feel the electricity he was causing, running through my veins. "Well, Nabi... Be a good girl for Daddy and use your words."

I looked up at him, giving him a devilish grin. "Yes Daddy, I am ready." My words made him groan out loud before he gradually pushed himself inside me, reassuring me I could change my mind at any stage. *Change my mind? Was this man mad?*

Damian finally stopped moving, allowing me some time to adjust to the size of him. He is definitely the biggest I had ever had, although my experience was limited.

Damian moaned so quietly I nearly missed it. "Fuck" The tone told me he was happy. "Fuck Nabi, your pussy was made for me, only me. You are so tight." He held himself off me, placing his arms either side of my head, " How do you feel? Need me to stop?" I couldn't help but giggle, "No, Daddy. I need you to start." A smile adorned his handsome face that went from one side to the other, " As my Butterfly wishes."

I felt him pull out of me slowly, he paused, staring at me so intensely as he shoved himself back in. He was right, I was made for him.

The way he pounded into me was possessive, he was claiming what was his and I was all for it. I knew in that moment that nothing like what had happened would happen again, not while Damian was with me.

Damian sat up on his knees as he fucked me and watched, he watched as I slid my hands up and over my breasts, squeezing them both tightly before pinching the nipples tightly and pulling them out towards Damian, moaning with pleasure as I did.

Damian slowed his rhythm. He started to take his time, enjoying what he was seeing. I felt his skin touch my clit and start to do soft circles. He knew exactly what a girl wanted and how to give it to her. His circle speed stayed steady with his body movements and the consistency was turning me on. I could feel myself getting closer and closer to the edge every time he slid himself back into me.

"God, Leah, you are so wet."

I gripped his back, digging my fingernails into his skin once again. Damian sucked in his breath and I knew he liked it. The knowledge brought a sly smirk to my face, and Damian didn't miss it.

"You think you are in charge now, huh?" He groaned, still fucking me with a steady rhythm.

"Let me show you who is actually in charge here," Damian grinned down at me and stopped moving, pulling his cock out of me, an action that my body seemed to hate since my automatic response was to groan 'no' outloud.

Laughing at me as he spoke, "Aw, don't worry baby, Daddy isn't planning on staying out of you for long." Grabbing my hips Damian flipped me over onto my stomach and lifted my ass into the air. His movements were precise, proving this wasn't his first time doing it.

I felt Damian grab my ass cheeks, squeezing them. Letting go after a minute he let one of his arms drop down and he wrapped the palm around his cock. I watched him through my legs as he touched himself.

"You like watching me play with myself, Nabi?" His question took me off guard and broke my concentration. Before his question had even entered my brain he continued, "Do you know how I know that?" I shook my head no. Damian's big hand came down on my ass, and I felt the goosebumps rise instantly.

He lightly brushed a finger over my clit, making me moan, then slid it inside me. His actions were slow and deliberate. The kind that left you feeling sexy.

He was so dominant and exuded power, but still so gentle and sweet had my body melting like it never had before.

This one experience had me learning things about myself I never knew and as far as I could tell, Damian had barely even started.

He took his finger away, replacing it with his cock, and once again he filled me. Stretching his arm down my back he grabbed my ponytail and pulled on it slightly, like he was asking me permission.

I sat up a little, arching my back with my ass up in the air while Damian pounded into me.

Pulling my hair even more I was forced to sit up on my knees, my back against his chest and his cock gliding in and out of me. The new position made me feel him inside me even more than I could before.

His free hand ran from my waist and up to my breast, squeezing it and gripping the nipple, pulling it out with a pinch. I moaned, he was getting me so worked up.

He placed his hand on my waist again and let go of my hair with the other before quickly moving it around my neck.

With the fingers of one of his hands applying pressure around my neck the other started to move from my waist until it found my clit.

I could feel my own juices running down my own legs and hitting the sheet.

"Oh fuck, Nabi." Damian groaned, pumping himself faster and faster into my pussy. I could hear him speaking through clamped teeth as he threw his head back and let go of my neck. "Touch yourself, Nabi. I'm going to stop touching you because I want you to take over…" He moved his other hand, having both of them now gripping my waist keeping me stable.

Reaching down I started rubbing my clit, I had never touched myself like this before. It was all new, having someone who wanted me to enjoy myself just as much as they wanted themselves to.

"Who's my whore? Hmm? My dirty little whore?" His words alone were the cherry on top and I exploded, coming everywhere. Damian however wasn't done, "Tell me, Nabi!" I knew he wanted me to answer his question… Moaning in a gravelly voice I managed to respond. "Me, I am your dirty little whore, Daddy."

That was all he needed, Damian came undone inside me. I could hear him panting behind me, then laughing. I turned around to see what he was laughing at, looking him in the eyes. "Jesus, Leah. You made quite the mess didn't you, Sweetheart?" I looked down on the bed to see it was absolutely saturated.

I felt Damian move his body off the bed and I looked back up at him to notice he had his hand reached out.

"C'mon princess, how about we jump in the shower and I clean you up?" Winking when he said clean. *Clean... sure....* I grinned as I took the hand he offered and he led me to the bathroom, knowing I was about to get more of what I just had and although I had my doubts about him, me... *us...* In this very moment I felt it was right... *We* are right.

CHAPTER 38

Leah's POV

As we stepped through the door frame of the bathroom, I looked around and it was like I was seeing it all for the first time. The walls I had thought were white suddenly showed the soft grey colour I had been told they were and the patterns in the tiles is something I had actually never noticed before.

For the first time, I am actually *seeing* my surroundings. I whipped my head around, facing the shower when I heard Damian turn on the water. Watching him as he stood there, arm stretched out feeling the temperature of what was raining down, making sure it was suitable.

I watched his arm flex, making his tattoos that covered it move, each one telling its own little story. Unconsciously, I reached out, gliding my fingertips over one that caught my eye. Damian turned his head slightly to look at me. "Does this one have a meaning?" I softly asked. Damian smiled at me, letting out a little chuckle.

"That was a drunken dare..." He trailed off like he was watching the memory play out through his mind, smiling and shaking his head slightly as he remembered.

He snapped himself back to reality, "It was all Markus's fault," He reached out and gripped onto my arms, sliding me closer to his naked body. Placing fingers under my chin he pushed my head upwards as he bent his neck and brushed his lips across mine. "I really don't want to think about my best friend right now, not that I can think about anything but what I am about to do to your very naked and very sexy body."

Damian kissed me, the soft and loving kisses were over and the demanding ones were here. I opened my mouth, allowing him to take whatever he wanted.

I could feel just how much he didn't want to think about Markus on my stomach. His fingers left their spot under my chin and I felt his arms wrap around my body, feeling their way down to my ass cheeks, squeezing them before he started to lift me up onto his body and walked us under the spray of the shower.

The water was still a little cold for me, but I didn't care. I just wanted this man to fuck me like he owned me. I was desperate to be his dirty little whore and I had no problems letting him know it as I grinded myself on his dick that was tucked up between us and pulled him in as close as I could with my legs wrapped around him.

His kisses were hard but gentle, letting me know how much he wanted this as well. He spun me around and my back hit the shower wall with a thud but I didn't even feel it, I was so engrossed with what was happening with this man.

Damian moved his lips from mine and moved to my ear, whispering, "I am going to fuck you now, Leah." I felt one of his hands let go of me and head south, I assumed to grab hold of his dick. My assumptions were confirmed when I felt the head rubbing on the entrance to my pussy. "Leah, Are you okay with this? Say the word and I will stop." His facial expression was serious. I pulled his ear close to my lips and softly spoke, "If you don't fuck me right now, I am going to have to go touch myself..." Pausing for dramatic effect before continuing on. "Without you being allowed in the room." I bit my lip, allowing the feeling I had of some kind of power over Damian to take over. I grinned at him with my bottom lip still between my teeth when he thrust himself into me. I gasped and held on to him, he pushed himself into me with every word, "You think you can tell me what to do?" He grabbed a fistfull of my hair and yanked it backwards, "Hmmm, Nabi?" His eyes had turned from the beautiful green colour to dark, almost black. It was like he was possessed. Surely he knew that this is exactly what I had intended. I felt the pleasure as it grew inside me, pulling myself closer and closer to his body, our skin rubbing against each other.

My moans started to get louder the faster he moved. "Do you like that hmm, Leah?" He quizzed, his cock moving hard and fast. I closed my eyes and nodded, moaning some form of an answer.

"Words. Use your words." He demanded. The tone in his voice surprised me and my eyes flung open. It was dark and demanding. He wasn't angry, it was power, he exuded it.

To prove to me how much power he held he stopped fucking me and placed me down, my feet hitting the wet tiles under us as I looked up at him. He smirked. I watched as his hand slid down his chest, grabbing his cock.

"On your knees, Leah." His demand was completed before his words had even fully registered, not taking my eyes off his once as I knelt down in front of him.

"MMmmmm." Damian moaned. "You are such a good girl, aren't you Nabi?" His hand started to glide up and down, the movement out of the corner of my eye drawing attention to it. I licked my lips, ready to get face fucked by this man.

He seemed to take forever so I took it upon myself to get us started. I rushed in and opened my mouth, allowing his dick to enter it. He was huge and long, I could feel the tip had precum on it as I slid it down the back of my throat groaning as my lips tightened around him.

"Oh fuck," Damian mumbled as he took each side of my head in his hands holding my head right where he wanted it. "You like my cock, don't you? Hmm??" I wanted to answer him but I didn't want to empty my mouth.

"You don't have to say anything Leah, I can tell how much you love it. You are my dirty little slut, aren't you?" Damian started moving, pleasuring himself with my mouth. Nice and slow in and out, making sure his dick hit the very back of my throat everytime making my gag reflex go crazy and my eyes water before suddenly removing himself from me entirely and standing me up. He spun me around and pushed me against the wall, squashing my breasts onto the cold tiles.

Holding my ass cheeks apart he slammed himself into me at the same time as he put his hand around my throat and squeezed.

He started pounding himself into my pussy as he tightened his grip around my neck and moved his other hand down to my clit gently rubbing circles.

He fucked me faster and faster and moved his hand at the same speed.

I could feel it starting to build and I felt like I was going to explode. I moaned loudly, "oh god, Daddy." Biting my lip to try and control myself before more words spilt from my mouth. "Fuck, I'm going to cum. Oh fuck, Damian I'm cumming." I felt myself let go and suddenly I saw fireworks, cumming like I never have before, the feeling so intense.

I didn't have a chance to float back down to earth as Damian continued to assault my clit with his fingers and my pussy with his cock, making me come a second time, this time taking him to see the fireworks with me.

I heard him groaning, "fuck, Leah." His pace started to slow down and I felt his cock start to soften inside me and suddenly it was quiet, the only sounds that could be heard was out breathing and the water pouring out of the shower.

After catching our breath Damian turned the water off and lifted me up into his arms. He walked us out of the shower, sitting me on the edge of the vanity as he walked over and got a dry towel for each of us. Wrapping me up in one of them he picked me up again, pulling me into his chest. I wrapped my legs around his waist and my arms around his neck, turning my head to the side and laying my cheek on his chest just above his pec.

Damian walked us to the living room and sat us on the lounge. I lifted my head and looked at him.

This man is so handsome, why, why did he choose me? I smiled as he brushed some hair behind my ear. "I love you, Leah." His voice was soft and gruff. I could feel his words in my soul, "I love you Damian." His smile widened and he bent in, gently kissing me, the kisses showing his love for me.

Damian's phone started ringing. He reached over, picking it up and answering it without looking at who was calling him.

"Yeah?" He said. I heard a woman's voice through the phone and I saw the smile fade from his face as he looked me dead in the eyes. I tried not to listen in but my ears pricked up when I heard her yelling that he had missed the ultrasound. *Ultrasound for what?*

The next words I heard threw me for six and was not something I suspected to hear.

"I didn't make this baby alone, Damian!!" My jaw dropped....

"Damian?" I softly spoke. He hung up instantly. "Damian, what's going on?" I questioned him. I was confused but also not confused, I know what I heard.

Damian looked away as he spoke, "Marisha is pregnant, she says it's mine."

Suddenly I couldn't breathe and the world went black.....

ACKNOWLEDGEME NTS:

Wren's Hens,
You guys are more than an editing and street team to me. You guys are family. Together we have now edited, promoted and released two books together and I couldn't imagine having to do this with anyone else. You allow me to do my thing while you guys take care of the hardest part, correcting all my mistakes. None of you will ever understand what you mean to me.
I love your faces!

Brandi & Randee:
My OG cheerleaders. Y'all always got my back, doesn't matter what the issue is. You will always give me the truth even if it is going to hurt me. I love you both so so much.

Mel, Megan and Heidi:
The three of us have been through it over the past 10 years, I am just grateful it was with you guys and not some weird cunt. Life is better with you guys in it.

Viv:
I would be lost without you. You have literally let me know when its peoples birthdays or when I have appointments. I love you more than I can ever tell you.

Gail:
Thank you for being you, for being right where I have always needed you. How did I get so lucky? I love you.

And my supporters...
From the Whole of my heart, thank you. Thank you for reading my books, thank you for supporting me and thank you for allowing me to take some of your time when you read my words.
xoxo

ABOUT THE AUTHOR:

TL Wren is an Australian Indie Author who released her first book Jackson Black during the height of the Covid pandemic. She is a wife and a mother and works a full time job as well as the writing.

You can find her stories on Inkitt, Wattpad and Ream Stories before they appear on Amazon.

Check out her socials, search TL Wren on Instagram, Facebook, Tik Tok, Twitter and Threads.